THE LEGEND OF BUDDY BUSH

THE
LEGEND OF
BUDDY
BUSH

SHELIA P. MOSES

MARGARET K. McELDERRY BOOKS
New York   London   Toronto   Sydney   Singapore

Margaret K. McElderry Books
An imprint of Simon & Schuster
Children's Publishing Division
1230 Avenue of the Americas
New York, New York 10020

Book design by O'Lanso Gabbidon

The text for this book is set in Bembo.
Printed in the United States of America

10 9 8

Library of Congress Cataloging-in-Publication Data
Moses, Shelia P.
The legend of Buddy Bush / Shelia P. Moses.—1st ed.
p. cm.
Summary: In 1947, twelve-year-old Pattie Mae is sustained by her dreams of escaping Rich Square, North Carolina, and moving to Harlem when her Uncle Buddy is arrest for attempted rape of a white woman and her grandfather is diagnosed with a terminal brain tumor.
ISBN 978-0-689-85839-0 (hardcover)
[1. Race relations—Fiction. 2. African Americans—North Carolina—Rich Square—Fiction. 3. Family life—North Carolina—Fiction. 4. Sick—Fiction. 5. Grandparents—Fiction. 6. Rich Square (N.C.)—Race relations-Fiction. 7. North Carolina—History—20th century-Fiction.]
I. Title.
PZ7.M8475Le 2004
[Fic]—dc21
2003008024

This book is dedicated to my beloved grandparents, Lucy and Braxton Jones, who gave my siblings and me a legacy to hold on to, and to their baby girl, my mother, Maless Moses, who passed the torch to their grandchildren.

CONTENTS

1	Thursday Letters	3
2	Dancing White Ladies	39
3	The Strawberry Patch	52
4	The Walk	57
5	Catfish Friday	67
6	The Queen's Chair	85
7	What a Time	101
8	The Amen Corner	105
9	Pretty Lady	109
10	Cloud Heads	125
11	Yellow	131
12	The Chain Gang	148
13	The Trial	162
14	Back to Harlem	172
15	The Law	178
16	Have You Ever Seen Cotton Grow?	186
17	The Train	203
	Author's Note	207
	Acknowledgments	214

June 5, 1947

Dear Pattie Mae,

How are you, Ma, Grandpa, and Grandma doing? I hope that this letter will find you all doing well. Tell them hello for me. I am fine and enjoying living in New York more and more each day. Harlem is more beautiful than anything you've ever seen on Grandma's new TV. Colored people are everywhere and they are dressed like they are going to Sunday go to meeting. Ma would die for one of the hats these ladies wear to church on Sunday morning. There are more cars on one block here than in all of Rich Square.

   I would tell you more, but I want you to see it with your own eyes. I got your letter about visiting me. Pattie Mae, when chopping season is over, I will send for you. Yes, little sister, come north with me and feel the freedom of these Northern colored folks.

Love, your big sister
BarJean

P.S. Tell Uncle Buddy hello, too.

1

Thursday Letters

*I*f you are reading this letter, you have found all my letters, all of my secrets. The secrets of Rehobeth Road and the secrets of Rich Square, North Carolina. Most of all, you know the truth about what happen to my uncle Goodwin "Buddy" Bush. Uncle Buddy wasn't really my uncle. He was what Grandpa called kinfolks on nobody's side. Just plain old kinfolks. Grandpa told me that Uncle Buddy had his own family a long time ago; a real ma and daddy. Blood kin! He was just staying with them while his folks Rosa Lee and Hersey worked in tobacco over in Rocky Mount. Rocky Mount ain't far, just north of the riverbank, about thirty-five miles from here. Grandpa said that Uncle Buddy's folks went to work one day and never made it back across that river. They were in some kind of accident in the tobacco barn and they both died on the same day. So my grandpa and grandma just kept Uncle Buddy and raised him like he was their own. He went North when he was sixteen. When he came back in 1942, he came home to us. I was seven years old. Blood kin or not there are few things about May 1, 1942, that I will ever forget. It was a Sunday when my uncle Buddy arrived. Ma let me stay home from church. My big sister and brother had to usher at church, so off they went. Me, I stayed home to lay eyes on him for the first time.

His car was blue.

Sky blue.

A Cadillac.

A new Cadillac.

His suit was blue too.

Dark blue.

With pinstripes.

Pinstripes like Grandpa's Sunday go to meeting suit.

I remember standing there holding my breath.

And my pee.

I couldn't leave that front porch.

The outhouse would just have to wait.

Lord, I wouldn't have missed that first sight at my uncle for nothing on Rehobeth Road.

A city man.

He pulled that Cadillac right up to Grandpa's front door.

I looked at his shiny shoes first. I could see my face in them.

I smiled.

My eyes went slowly up his legs.

They looked so long.

His jacket had

one

two

three

let's see

six buttons.

His shirt was white.

His tie was a pinstripe like his suit.

Then I saw the hat.

I will never forget that hat.

Yes, blue with a feather to the right.

Only a city man could own a hat like that.

Grandpa stood beside me.

He never moved.

I stepped to the right.

Grandpa waited for Uncle Buddy to walk up to him.

He did.

"Welcome home, son."

"It's good to be home, Daddy Braxton."

They hugged.

Grandpa looked over his shoulder at the Cadillac.

"Nice car, boy."

"Oh, it ain't much."

Ma runs onto the front porch.

"Ain't much! Bro, I ain't never seen a car this fancy, never."

"Hey, sister." He smiled a big smile at Ma as she ran around his car.

She rubbed it like it was a genie bottle. Then she ran over to Uncle Buddy and jumped in his arms like she was a rag doll.

"Hey, Bro."

That only left Grandma to welcome Uncle Buddy home.

"Come on in this house, boy. I been keeping your breakfast warm all mornin'."

We all followed Uncle Buddy inside.

I saw Grandma cry for the first time when she hugged her only boy. The one that ain't blood kin.

We ate.

We laughed.

We had a time.

We were a family.

I wonder if Uncle Buddy was thinking about his real folks that day. I hope he wasn't sad. They must have loved him so, but Lord knows we love him too. I can't imagine anybody loving him more than Grandpa did. More than me! I am glad he is my uncle and I wish he would come back to us. But he can't because there still ain't no telling what white folks might try to do to him. I don't think Uncle Buddy will ever be able to come home again, so I just wrote about him in my letters to BarJean and on paper sacks around the house. When I was done writing the letters I mailed some of them to my big sister. Some of them, I hid in the old smokehouse in the backyard. Yes, I hid the truth. A lot of truth is hidden around here. If only the trees could talk or the dirt could sing.

I remember like it was yesterday when this whole mess that forced Uncle Buddy to leave us started. Sometimes when I think about what happened, I feel twelve again. That's how old I was in June of 1947. I'm telling you I can just relive it like it's happening now. Right now.

This June morning is no different than any other hot summer day on Rehobeth Road. The moon was full last week and I'm sure it is about to change all our lives, just as my grandma said full moons do. Last year when the full moon came my grandma said she saw death in that moon. Surely enough my cousin June Bug, my aunt Rosie's boy, who was only ten, went ice-skating with no skates over on Jackson Creek. Well the ice was too thin and both June Bug and his cousin Willie on his daddy side fell in and drowned. They held a double funeral for them and everybody was crying.

Sad . . .

Sad . . .

Now every time a full moon comes, I just get scared, scared, scared. When the full moon came last week, I thought old man death would surely be back for another one of us.

To my knowledge every one of us with Jones blood are up this June morning clothed in our right mind. So I pray the full moon won't bring no sorrow this time. I'm up early to pick cucumbers. It's Friday and the heavens opened last night and let out enough rain for Ma to announce that we wouldn't be going in the cotton field to chop today. We chop for Ole Man Taylor, who owns this land, this house, and most of Rehobeth Road. His great-great-granddaddy owned all of this land during slavery. He lets Ma plant whatever she wants on the land that he don't use. Working our crops, not his, suits me just fine as I happily roll out of the bed. Softly, my feet touch the old sack that we use as a rug. Soft enough for me to not wake up Ma, who is sleeping across the kitchen in what we call Ma's room. My room is the girls' room, because that's where my sister BarJean and me slept together when she lived at home. Her real name is Barbara Jean, but no one is called by their real name on Rehobeth Road. That includes me, who would prefer Patricia to Pattie Mae any day. There's a boys' room upstairs next to Uncle Buddy's room. That's where my big brother Coy, whose real name is McCoy, slept until he moved up North at sixteen back in 1945. So I guess it ain't nobody's room right now.

BarJean moved up North last year and she said she ain't never living in these sticks again, never. So I guess this ain't the girls' room no more, it's my room.

When I was really little, we all slept upstairs in this big old brown house. Not one drop of paint on it. By looking at it no one would ever know that rich white folks lived here first. When it was white, this house was the main house of the plantation. After the white folks left, the slaves moved in. That's why we call it the slave house. But it was surely a plantation main house first. Taylor's Plantation. It's still carved on a silver bell that's hanging from a tree in the backyard. Big letters—TAYLOR'S PLANTATION. Ma said during slavery that bell was used for ringing at feeding time. Not the animals, the slaves. I think that old bell is worth some money because Mr. Spivey, who owns the antique store over in Scotland Neck, has been trying to get Ma to sell him that bell for years. Ma told him, "You know I don't own this house, so I shoo don't own that bell. You need to ask Ole Man Taylor." Mr. Spivey ain't going to ask that mean man nothing, so that bell just hanging there reminding us of slavery.

Maybe revenge is sweet because my grandpa, Braxton Jones, who lives right down the road on his own land, said that the Yankees ran all them white folks away after the Civil War. He said the Taylors didn't come back for years to claim this land. My grandma, Babe Jones, said, "Braxton don't know what he's talking about because he wasn't even born then." Grandpa said, "No, I wasn't born, but I knows what my pappy Ben Jones told me." I don't know who's right and who's wrong, but Uncle

Buddy said, "It don't matter because don't nobody but poor-ass niggers want this raggedy damn house now."

He better not let Ma hear him say that after she let him move in with us when I was seven. Yep, right after breakfast the day Uncle Buddy arrived, he came home with us and never left. When he moved in, Ma packed all our stuff and moved us downstairs on top of each other like sardines in a can. Everybody except Coy. Just because he is a boy, he got to stay upstairs. There was plenty room upstairs for all of us. Ma says every day that God sends, that it don't look right to folks here on Rehobeth Road for her to be sleeping upstairs with a man that ain't blood kin. Raised in the same house and she talking about he ain't blood kin. But she said Uncle Buddy is more than welcome here, because he gives her $35.00 a month for rent and food. That money goes a long way because he doesn't eat here much. As a matter of fact, Uncle Buddy ain't hardly here at all. He's up at 4:00 and out the door by 5:00. Off to the sawmill in town where he been working since he arrived. He is the only colored at Quick's Sawmill. I don't think the white folks there like him very much, because he said they think all coloreds belong in the cotton field.

He told me the only cotton he picking is his T-shirt up off the floor. Uncle Buddy works half a day on Saturday, but he always hangs around in town to wait for me so we can have meat skins biscuits together while Grandma gets her grocery. That's the only day a week I get to go into town other than school days. I am Grandma's official grocery helper. She doesn't know it, but Grandpa gives me a quarter every week for going with her. Grandpa doesn't know it, but I would go for free just to be with Grandma and to go into town.

I best stop thinking about town and my quarter and get myself in that cucumber patch. I get myself past Ma. Past the old breakfast table with chairs that don't match and out the door. I close it with ease and Ma never move. It don't seem like nobody up on Rehobeth Road but me and my dog Hobo. Uncle Buddy gave him to me four years ago. He found him wandering around at the sawmill.

Nobody claimed him for a month and he became my dog.

I don't want to explain to Ma why I am trying to get these cucumbers off the vines so early. Ma thinks it ain't never too hot to work. I prefer not to get too black, myself. But that ain't my only reason for trying to beat the sun today. I want to finish my cucumbers and help Grandma with her strawberries all before 4 o'clock. That way I can rest before going into town with Uncle Buddy for my first picture show tonight. That's right. We are going to the movie house for the first time in my life. My clothes are all laid out on the bed down the road at Grandma and Grandpa's. I took them yesterday so I will be ready tonight. I'm wearing my blue and yellow checked skirt and my blue top. I hope Ma don't say nothing about me wearing my Sunday go to meeting shoes on a Friday night. She definitely will, so I better get ready to hear her fuss. Uncle Buddy and me will be leaving right after supper. First things first. I got to get these cucumbers picked.

As I lean over to pick my first one, I remember the stick that Uncle Buddy made for me to use to push the vines back. I keep it hidden on the third row. That's my row to pick, so I know Ma won't find it. Nothing fancy, just a stick with a hoop on the end. Uncle Buddy said I was going to ruin my hands if I don't stop working like a 1947 slave on this farm. If that happens, according to Uncle Buddy my chances of becoming a city girl are over. We talk about the North all the time. No matter if he was born here, my uncle Buddy is a New York man and you can tell it when he talks. He ain't all-countrified like me and the rest of the folks on Rehobeth Road. He's dress different even when he's going to work. You could never know Uncle Buddy ain't blood kin. He is tall like Grandpa and Coy; and as black as midnight. I've never seen teeth as white as his. And don't nobody in Rich Square shine their shoes like he does. "You can tell a real man by the shoes he wears," Uncle Buddy declares at least once a week. And he don't believe in the country stuff we believe in, like getting off the sidewalk to let white folks pass by. Uncle Buddy don't even believe in hanks. Folks on Rehobeth Road call ghost hanks. Uncle Buddy call ghost ghost and he don't believe in them either. Yep, he's a city man all right. For the life of me I will never understand why he came back five years ago. Nobody knows for sure. He just showed up that Sunday morning after writing a letter and didn't say why he was coming or why he won't be going back. BarJean claims she know, but I don't think she know nothing. She claims some folks in Harlem said Uncle Buddy left because he could not have the woman he loved. A woman that belonged to somebody else. A light-skin woman! She claim Uncle Buddy heart was broken. I can't imagine going North for twenty-two years, then moving back here. I definitely would not leave because I could not have some man. I would just find me a new one. That's what Uncle Buddy should have done. Found him a new woman to love. A dark-skin woman! Anything except come back here. I live and dream of the day when I leave this place and go to New York. Not just New York, but to Harlem. Not even Ma can get into my dreams.

"Pattie Mae!"

Guess I spoke too soon.

That would be Ma. Trying her best to get into my dreams; yelling like I'm halfway cross the field somewhere.

"Mornin' Ma."

"Mornin' my foot, what you doing in that field so early?"

I want to yell back, "Trying on my new diamond earrings."

Ma ain't much on people joking with her so I better not say that.

"Just trying to beat the sun."

"Trying to beat the sun. Child, you can't outrun God. You better stop listening to Buddy about that light-skin, dark-skin mess. Now come on this porch and wash your hands while I finish breakfast. I already put water in the face tub."

Lord, when I get to Harlem I'll be done with using face tubs. BarJean told me she got running water and yes, a bathroom. I put my stick down and Hobo and me slowly walk back to the slave house. I don't know who use to live in it, but I know I feel like a slave this morning. Just look at this place, all run down. But Ma keeps it so nice and clean. Cleaner than them white folks' yards in town. Probably cleaner on the inside too. They just got paint on the inside and the outside. This place ain't seen no paint since the Civil War. The closer I get to the slave house I want to scream, "I hate these fields. Please, BarJean, take me North!" By the time I make it to the porch Ma has turned around and gone inside. But not before I notice she is wearing a dress. I hope that I will be as tall as she is when I'm a woman. I saw on some of her important papers that she is six feet tall. Tall and beautiful with skin the color of a brown paper sack and hair that has as many waves in it as a newborn baby. When Ma walks, all the men look at her hips that are round and shake like Jell-O. Mr. Walter Garris likes Ma's hips so much that he screams, "Lord have mercy!" when she walks by. That makes Ma really mad. Uncle Buddy says I am going to be a pretty woman like Ma when I get older. He says probably not as pretty as Ma, because it's a "Sin-fore God to look as good as Mer Sheals." Her name is Mary. Somebody replaced the "a" with an "e" and dropped the "y" years ago, just like they took "tricia" off of Patricia and added "tie Mae" to my name. That's just how it is on Rehobeth Road.

So why is Ma wearing a dress? Surely she is going to pick cucumbers today. She always picks cucumbers when it rains. If she ain't chopping, she picks cucumber every day from late May until they are all gone, from sunrise to sunset. Ma stops chopping in August in time to work in tobacco, because tobacco workers make $4.00 a day and we only make $2.00 a day chopping. But August nor tobacco are on my mind this year, because I will be on that train going to the unknown by then. This will be the first year that I am old enough to work in the tobacco field, like it is honor or something stupid like that to turn twelve and prime tobacco. That's the rule on Rehobeth Road. You have to be twelve to work in the tobacco field. Myself, Pattie Mae Sheals, has other plans. Besides, Uncle Buddy says people who chop and prime tobacco ain't nothing but $2.00 a day slaves.

I stop on the back porch and wash my hands in the white face tub that Ma left there for me. Old like everything else around here. Clean like everything else around here. The smell of her biscuits reaches my nose before I reach the back door that is falling off the way it does at least ten times a week. I'm sure Grandpa is coming up here with his toolbox and fix it as soon as he gets around to it. He has been a bit under the weather, so I don't want to mention the door to him again. No need to tell Uncle Buddy because it's dark when he leaves home and dark when he comes back. Ma never complains about what Uncle Buddy don't do around here. I guess that $35.00 a month includes Ma fixing things too. Ma swears that money keeps us out of the poorhouse. If this ain't the poorhouse, I don't know what is.

Inside the slave house, in the kitchen, on the table I notice Ma's black leather bag. The one that her oldest sister, my aunt Louise, brought her all the way from Harlem. I also notice that Ma doesn't have on just any dress; she has on her Sunday go to meeting dress. She would never dress like this during the week, unless she was going to a funeral or the relief office over in Jackson. Lord have mercy, I just want to ask her why she is all dressed up, but

Ma says that children ain't suppose to ask grown folks questions.

That's another rule on Rehobeth Road. "Don't ask grown folks no questions."

I know I really don't have to. All I have to say is "Ma, you look so pretty." And she does. Even if she don't, Uncle Buddy says never beg a woman. "If you tell her she looks good, she will tell you anything you want to know." Stuff like "Honey, honey you fine as you want to be" and "Baby, you the sugar in my coffee." Now that's the kind of mess Uncle Buddy says he used to tell them gals up in Harlem. I don't know about them city women that Uncle Buddy knows, but Ma loves a compliment. So I just take my seat at the end of the table, next to the stove, where I have been sitting since Ma took me out of the high chair. The high chair we sold back to the thrift shop in Jackson when I got too big for it. Ma has prepared the usual two eggs, two pieces of bacon, and one biscuit. No milk, just water from the rusty well in the backyard.

"My, you look pretty today, Ma."

"Well, thank you, child. I thought I would get

dressed early. Mr. Charlie will be here soon."

Ma would not be dressed like this just because Mr. Charlie is coming by. He comes by all the time. Mr. Charlie and his wife, Miss Doleebuck, are Grandpa and Grandma's neighbors and best friends. At seventy-five, the same age as Grandpa, Mr. Charlie has a car. A 1935 Chevy. That's it. The car! Mr. Charlie and Ma are going somewhere, but I have to find out where.

"I told you to eat your food. Mr. Charlie will be here in a minute. Now hurry."

"He will?" I say, trying not to ask a grown folks question.

"Yes he will. I'm going into town with him and your grandpa. He's taking Poppa to see Dr. Franklin."

"Doctor?"

No time to follow some silly rule about not asking grown folks questions. I want to know why Grandpa is going to the doctor.

"Why?" I ask as tears run into the eggs that I don't want no more.

I know Ma is getting ready to say, "Don't ask

grown folks questions," until she sees the tears in my eggs.

"Now why are you crying, child? You know Poppa hasn't been feeling well for a while. And what did Buddy tell you about crying all the time?" If I tell her what he really said she would give him a tongue-lashing as soon as he steps foot in this house. But what he really said was "Crying makes you piss less." I can't repeat that, so I say, "He said big girls don't cry."

Ma smiles and say, "He's right. Now, hurry."

Ma's mighty out of herself this morning. She just rushing and fussing. She must be some kind of worried about Grandpa. He is definitely a little under the weather, but he must be really sick to go to a doctor. I figure that he has drunk enough of Grandma's leaves from the woods to feel better by now. Grandma claims she has a cure for everything. Puttin' tobacco on your chest for a sore throat. A penny around your neck to stop a nosebleed. A broom at the door so the hanks won't ride your back at night and roots from the grass of the unknown for colds. And she has birthed as many babies in Rich Square as Dr. Franklin, the white doctor. She brought BarJean, Coy and me into this world and most of the children here on Reheboth Road. She nurses most of the grown folks on Rehobeth Road too, except Uncle Buddy. He says, "Never in this world." As a matter of fact, Uncle Buddy don't trust no doctors around here. He drives all the way to Harlem twice a year to see his city doctor. There have been a lot of talk on Rehobeth Road about a new colored doctor coming to town. Not Rich Square, but Potecasi and that ain't too far. I guess that place is about ten miles away. Can't worry about a colored doctor that might come later. I want Ma to tell me about the white doctor that's here now and why Grandpa is really going to see him.

Ma still in deep thought, she doesn't say a word for a minute.

"Ma, I guess Grandma's medicine ain't working." I'm trying my best to get her to talk. She looks like she wants to laugh at my belief in Grandma's homemade medicine. Like the time I couldn't stop pissing in the bed and she boiled me some green stuff to drink for a month. Ma said that it wasn't that stuff that worked. She is probably right and it was her threats of beating my skin off if I didn't stop messing up her sheets that did. I just didn't understand why Ma went through all the pain of having me and then she planned to beat my skin off. Anyway, I want to know what is happening with Grandpa. My grandpa!

"Don't you worry about Grandpa. He just has a slight cold."

I can't believe she just said that.

A churchwoman lying. Lord have mercy!

"Slight cold? It's June."

Ma ignores me as she takes her old blue apron off and hangs it on a nail behind the kitchen door that don't have paint on it either. Then she sits down and takes off her bedroom slippers and puts on her black Sunday go to meeting shoes.

"Can I go with you to town? I want to see Grandpa."

"No you cannot. You have to go and help your grandma pick strawberries. She is waiting for you."

Grandma's strawberry patch is as big as our

cucumber patch and she sales them at the market every other Saturday as fast as we pick them. Sometimes folks, even white folks, come by the house to buy them by the basket. She only charges a dollar a basket. I overheard Uncle Buddy telling Grandma she should charge more for her big, pretty strawberries. She quickly told him he should mind his business. "Folks round here don't have that city money like you made in Harlem, boy."

End of that!

Ma reaches in her bag and pulls out my letter from BarJean that probably arrived yesterday, but she forgot to give it to me. She forgets sometimes and I have to ask for my Thursday's mail. Rain, sleet, or snow, my letters come from BarJean every Thursday that the Lord sends. Always on blue stationery in a blue envelope and always on Thursday. As she gives me the letter, I hear Mr. Charlie's car horn blowing like he is running from a fire.

Before Ma can say, "Sit back down and eat," I grab my letter, stuff it in my pocket, and run out of the door. Surely, she is not going to forget that I grabbed that letter out her hand. That will get me one lick or no TV at Grandma's house for a week. Don't have to worry about the TV around here. We don't have one. Uncle Buddy says he don't care what Ma says, he's giving me a TV for Christmas.

Mr. Charlie is waving as I run down the long path trying to get to the car before Ma can even get her purse off the table. I want a minute alone with two of my three favorite men. Uncle Buddy is the third, of course. Actually they are the only men in my life. Uncle Buddy said my daddy, Silas Sheals, ran off with Mr. Charlie's gal Mattie when I was a baby. He also said that my daddy and Mattie got themselves a new baby girl named O'Hara. Named after that white woman Scarlett O'Hara from *Gone with the Wind*. Ma don't ever say nothing about my daddy and Mr. Charlie and Grandpa somehow managed to stay friends. Now Miss Doleebuck dares my daddy to dot in her door and the same goes for Mattie if she wants to bring him with her. So Mattie only comes on holidays and Silas Sheals don't show his face at all. Miss Doleebuck said they both are a disgrace. Grandma said, "Disgrace my foot, Mattie is a slut." I'm almost sure that

Grandma is going to tell me what a slut is as soon as I am older.

I tell you one thing, if she don't tell me, Uncle Buddy will. All I got to do is ask him.

I pull the car door open and jump in Grandpa's lap.

"Hey, gal," he and Mr. Charlie say at the same time.

"Hey, Mr. Charlie. Hey, Grandpa."

Grandpa don't look the way he did yesterday. He is dark compared to his light skin that usually look like a cake of butter from their old cow that I named Sue. The poor cow was nine years old and didn't even have a name until last year. Rooms on Rehobeth Road got names, why can't the cows?

"Are you okay, Grandpa?"

"I'm all right, child. How you this mornin'?"

"I'm fine. I got up really early today."

"Is that so? And why did you do that?"

"Well the ground too wet to chop, but I picked a basket of cucumbers. I'm trying to sell a lot so that I will have extra money when I go North. Uncle

Buddy said there's lots of stuff to buy in Harlem."

"He did, did he? And just where is Buddy this morning?"

"Working as usual. But he is taking me to the movie house tonight."

Grandpa said he was never going to that theater as long as colored folks have to go in the back door. But he is glad that I am going.

"Well, that will be nice."

"You aren't going anywhere if you don't get your tail off of Poppa so that we can leave."

The voice of trouble have caught up with me.

Ma has made it down our long path and she looks so pretty as she give me the look.

"Leave her alone, Mer. She just saying good mornin'."

Thank God, Grandpa is coming to my defense. Not that Ma is listening. She says Grandpa can't raise her children. Now she says that to me, not to Grandpa. She don't do no talking back to Grandma or Grandpa even if she is forty-eight.

"Fine, but we have to go." Now she's giving me the "I'm going to tear your tail up later" look.

I ease out of the car and stand on the wet grass hoping Ma will let me go.

Instead she starts giving me orders for the rest of the day.

"Now you know you can't stay home by yourself. Go on up to Ma Babe's and I will come there when we leave Dr. Franklin's."

That's what Ma call my grandma, "Ma Babe."

"But I haven't taken my bath yet."

"You don't need a bath. You are going straight to the strawberry patch."

"Bye," I say as I wave.

They wave back as Ma points her finger, saying something. Who knows what. I will have to talk to Ma later when Grandpa and Mr. Charlie ain't around. I know she knows I'm becoming a woman and I'm getting too old not to wash up before leaving home. I don't know when, but soon I know I'm going to get my period just like Denise and Sylvia at school did. Denise told me she was sick as a dog when Mother Nature came to visit her the first time. Sylvia said she didn't hurt at all. Accordingly to the conversation I overheard between BarJean and her best friend Boogie, Miss Doleebuck's granddaughter, the only reason Sylvia didn't hurt when she got her first period is because she had been messing with boys already. What a horrible thought. I think Sylvia might be a slut, too, like Mattie. Denise, Sylvia and me suppose to be best friends at school. But I like Caroline much better than both of them. We call her Chick-A-Boo. She lives right down the road. She is my real best friend. Those other girls are not like us. They are town people. They got more than two pairs of shoes and they have daddies. Beside, they spend all their time talking about boys. Uncle Buddy has already warned me to stay away from boys. He said they will give me worms. God forbid what that means.

I just pray we move into a house with a bathroom before my period comes. I don't want to use the outhouse for such personal matters. But I'll worry about my period when it comes.

Right now I just want Grandpa to get well. I feel like crying just thinking about Grandpa going to the doctor. Specially Dr. Franklin. Now Grandpa don't know that I know this, but one day when I was fishing with Uncle Buddy over in Jackson Creek, he told me that Dr. Franklin and his brother Eddie, who is the sheriff, had mistreated Grandpa about thirty-five years ago. See, before the Holy Ghost came and saved Grandpa one Sunday morning at Chapel Hill Baptist Church where he has been attending for fifty years, he would go into town and drink in what colored folks called "the bottom" on Saturday nights. It was really an alley where the colored men would get together every Friday and Saturday night to play cards and enjoy their moonshine. Grandpa said he had a mason jar of moonshine too many when he decided to go home before Grandma came looking for him.

Just as he tried to climb into his old pickup truck, the sheriff stopped him.

"Where you going, boy?"

"Home, Sheriff Franklin. Just heading home."

"Not tonight, you ain't!"

Grandpa was more than willing to sleep the moonshine off in jail. But that old mean sheriff took it upon himself to hit Grandpa over the head with his billy club before arresting him. Knocked Grandpa cold and threw him in jail. Uncle Buddy said Grandpa was convinced that Dr. Franklin, whose office was upstairs from the jail, knew he was hurt and didn't come to see about him until morning. Both them Franklin boys are mean. Now if Grandpa even mentions their names, he'll say, "Yes, evil and evil sleep in the same bed."

When Dr. Franklin finally checked on Grandpa just before day, he wrapped his head in some bandages and let him drive himself home. Well it turned out Grandpa had a brain concussion (whatever that is) and he drove his old red Ford right into a tree down on Brown Hill Road. Grandpa passed out and slept for hours. By seven in the morning, Grandma and Miss Doleebuck headed out on foot searching for their husbands. Yes, Mr. Charlie was in the cell next to Grandpa the night before for no reason at all. They just arrested him for coming to the jail to look for Grandpa.

They released Mr. Charlie later on that day when Boogie's mama, Fannie Mae, went down to that jail and cussed them out like they weren't even white folks. Around 8:30 that morning, Grandma and Miss Doleebuck made it to Grandpa's truck where he was still passed out. It took them a while to wake him up, and when they did they had to walk all the way home. Poor Grandpa started having blackouts after that and he never took another sip of moonshine. Been saved and sober ever since.

The other thing Grandpa don't know is Uncle Buddy told me that although he was little he remember the whole thing. He also don't know that Uncle Buddy and some of his friends, Lennie, Hosea, and Earl, went out to town that next weekend and put holes in every Franklin car tire that they would find. They sure did. That's what Uncle Buddy said and I believe him. Mercy to the highest, it's nice to have all this grown folks business at twelve.

I better stop thinking about all of this before I reach Jones Property because Grandma can read your mind. Now she is a piece of work. I swear that woman knows what I am thinking before I do. Smoke coming from the chimney in the kitchen at

Grandma's house and I know she has not put out the breakfast fire yet. Thank God, she'll cook me some breakfast, I'm thinking, as I walk faster. I can't make it till noon without food.

That pleasant thought ends quickly when I find myself face to face with the bulls from Mr. Bay's dairy. He is Grandpa and Grandma's neighbor and compared to us, Mr. Bay is a rich man. Rich and mean. I don't think he like colored folks very much and he laughs every time one of us forget and wear red while passing his terrifying bulls. Today that would be me. There is a big fence between me and the bulls, but I am still afraid to run, because I know they will run all the way down the fence with me. That alone scares me to death. Uncle Buddy walks by here whenever he wants to, wearing blue, red, whatever colors he please. He says, "I ain't scared of no damn bull. I'm going to eat them for dinner one day. They ain't going to eat me."

I can't run if I want to since my dear sweet ma locked me out of the house in my bare feet. I want to stick my tongue out, but that's red too.

I walk in slow motion as the mama cows join the

bulls at the edge of the dairy farm field. There must be fifty all together.

I finally reach the path that divide Mr. Bay's dairy from Jones Property. I am still nervous when I reach in my pockets and feel my new letter from BarJean. The bulls have scared me so bad that I almost forgot I had it. I stop at the pecan tree to catch my breath and to read my letter. Grandpa planted this tree forty-eight years ago for Ma. The day she was born. He calls it Mer's tree. In the back there are trees for her sisters, the Louise tree and the Rosie tree. Yes, Uncle Buddy has a tree too, right over there at the pond. Since he ain't blood kin, Grandpa just took Uncle Buddy for a walk when he was ten and let him pick out his own tree on Jones Property. The day I was born Ma said Grandpa went right outside and planted my tree. But the Pattie Mae tree ain't big enough to sit under yet. So I'll just set under Mer's tree to read my letter.

The paper is blue like always and it smells like BarJean's favorite perfume. I can hardly wait to sit down as Hobo, who has followed me all the way, lies down beside me. The words make me feel closer to the North that I will soon see.

Dear Pattie Mae:

How are you, Ma, Grandpa, Grandma, and Uncle Buddy doing? I am doing fine and so is Coy. You know we have been sharing an apartment together all year. Well, the big day has come and I am moving into my own place down on 125th Street. Your big brother has met a really nice girl and they are getting married. That's right! Now you will have two big sisters.

Guess what? Her name is Mary, just like Ma's. Isn't that nice?

Now you have to keep this whole marriage thing a secret and not tell Ma. Coy wants to tell her himself. So be a big girl and don't tell her. Okay?

My dear little sister, I'm glad you want to come here in late August.

I have to go now and I am looking forward to seeing you soon. You, my dear sister, will be my first guest in my new apartment.

Love, your big sister
BarJean

Coy is going to get married! More importantly, BarJean trust me enough to tell me a secret.

I put my letter back in my pocket and tuck my secret in the back of my mind. At least until I see Grandpa. I'll tell him and he will tell no one. Difference from me.

I stick my tongue out at the bulls that are far away now and start walking as fast as my legs can carry me to get me some breakfast.

2

Dancing White Ladies

I can smell Grandma's biscuits as I get closer to the steps that Grandpa built with his bare hands. Their house is painted white with green trimming around the windows. Yes, my grandpa painted the house. He tried to get Old Man Taylor to let him paint our house, too. Ole Man Taylor said no and Grandpa ain't spoke to that white man since then. Grandpa's cat, Hudson, meets me at the door. He and Hobo sure ain't friends. They fight like . . . Well, they fight like cats and dogs. I open the back door that's painted green too, and there she is. My grandma. The woman of the house. And everybody that walks in this door knows that. She ain't no taller than I am. Black, as Grandpa is yellow. Her hair the same color as the

silver quarters that Uncle Buddy gave me to save.
He said that Grandma is what men folks call
"black gal pretty."

"Good mornin', Grandma. How are you feeling
today?"

I know the answer before she even answers. All
my life I have asked her the same question and get
the same answer.

"Child, Grandma don't feel so good today."

She just loves saying it, like it was a hymn she
and Ma sang in the choir on Sunday morning. No
matter how many times you ask, she gives you the
same answer. When BarJean and Coy were at
home with me, each of us asked the same question
and got the same answer. Ma would skin us alive if
one of us run in and just said "Hey." We had to line
up like soldiers ready to salute our commander and
ask her how she was doing. Then we stood there
and waited for her to answer. I still have to do the
ritual. Sometimes it takes Grandma five minutes to
answer. Sometimes ten, if she really ain't feeling so
good. Whatever the time, you just stand there and
wait.

Grandpa said that was Grandma's way of controlling us. He and Mr. Charlie use that word "control" a lot when they are talking about their wives. They said them two live to tell other folks what to do. I guess they are controlling Grandpa and Mr. Charlie too, because they don't ever say that mess about the women loud enough for the women to hear them.

I wish I were grown so I could do like Uncle Buddy does when he comes in Grandma's house. He don't ask her nothing. He just says, "Ma Babe, you shoo looking good today." He said he ain't asking her nothing, because he might die waiting for an answer. "Besides," he said, "ain't nothing wrong with a woman who can pick two bushels of strawberries a day. Nothing."

I wait as Grandma wipes her hands in the end of her apron and start thinking about when she might tell me how she's feeling. First, she takes out her breakfast dishes and puts them on the table. One by one, she pulls out the white plates with the dancing white ladies on them. I want her to hurry up because I can't tell her I cried in my eggs and didn't finish eating my breakfast until after she finish her ritual.

Finally the words come. "Child, Grandma don't feel so good today."

There, she said it.

"Oh, I'm sorry, Grandma. What's wrong?"

"Nothing special, just old age I guess. How are you this mornin'?"

"I'm okay. Just hungry."

"What you doing hungry, child? Didn't Mer fix you breakfast?"

"Well, she did, but I didn't get to finish because Mr. Charlie came to get her."

I start praying immediately that Grandma will forget the lie that I just told and don't tell Ma. The last time Ma caught me in a lie she wore my behind out with a plastic cake-mixing spoon. Grandma don't look like she believe me. But she never could stand the sight of a hungry man, woman, or child. "Never mind, just sit down and let Grandma fix you someteat."

That's her word for something to eat. I don't dare correct her or any of the old folks on Rehobeth

Road. We all understand what they mean. Besides Uncle Buddy swears that them old folks are a lot smarter than us schoolchildren. They have their own words, like "dor" for "door," "yes-ciddie" for "yesterday," "yonder" for "over there," and "boot" for "car trunk."

Right now all I need is someteat and some information about Grandpa.

"Grandma, can I ask you a grown folks question?"

"Depends on what it is."

"Well, what's wrong with Grandpa and why didn't you go with him to the doctor?"

Grandma sits down and pours herself another cup of coffee from the white and blue teakettle that's almost black from fire that comes out of the potbelly stove that she loves so dearly. She doesn't even use milk and that means she needs something strong to help her through the day. Before I know it, Grandma is standing up and getting an extra saucer with white ladies dancing on it out of the cupboard. I'm so happy because I know that I am going to get a saucerful of coffee. "Our little secret, of course," Grandma says. She's the only person on Rehobeth Road that thinks that I am old enough to have at least a taste of coffee. Grandpa and Ma said that coffee makes children crazy. When I told Uncle Buddy what they said, he said, "That's the craziest damn mess I ever heard." Now I ain't old enough to curse, but I know he is right about that being the craziest mess we ever heard.

I was getting ready to sit down when I notice that Grandma got herself a new kitchen set.

"Why, Grandma, you have a new table and chairs."

"Yes, I do. Ain't it nice?"

"Yes, it's real nice, but when did it come? I didn't see the Sears truck pass our house."

"That's because it didn't come from Sears. Now don't get me wrong, ain't nothing the matter with their furniture. But I have always wanted to order me something out of that Helig Myers catalog that Doleebuck gets in the mail."

I can't believe it. Furniture from Helig Myers. New furniture.

I rub my hand along the table and think about

how many Helig Myers stores they must have in New York.

"This is really nice, Grandma."

"Thank you, child. Your grandpa bought it for me. He finally sold the lumber off of them ten acres of land back of the field and this is what we got with some of the money. Not only that, we have some left to hide under the house for hard times." That's one thing about my grandfolks I learned at an earlier age. They know how to save money. I also learned that Grandpa don't never stay away from home at night because under his house is a hole. In that hole is a jar. In that jar is money. I have seen Ma crawl under there on her hands and knees many nights while Grandpa hold the nightlight. Don't nobody go in that jar but Ma. Nobody! She writes down how much goes in and how much goes out. She is Grandpa's right hand when it comes to business. That's just fine with Grandma. She keeps what she needs right in her bra. Every now and then she will get extra for things she wants or needs.

Like this new table and chairs.

Grandpa told me to get myself a jar. He said, "The money you save today will save you tomorrow." When I save enough money I can buy me something nice like Grandma bought herself.

I don't know if she is prouder of the table or the property they own. Grandpa is one of the few colored men in Rich Square that own his own land. Most of the people rent their houses and land from some of the white folks, who will let you stay as long as you don't get uppity and try to do something sensible like speak up for yourself. Ma rents from Old Man Taylor and she don't care what he say. She says whatever she wants when she wants to. I don't have to tell you that Uncle Buddy does too. Since he only give Ma $35.00 a month, he said he is saving enough money to build his own house. He says he has waited all his life to buy a place, just to tell white folks to "get off my damn land." When he does get him a house he says he's going to let us live with him. "Good-bye, slave house," he'll say. I hope he builds it nearby. I have to be able to sit on the porch with Grandpa half the evening and with Uncle Buddy the other half.

Grandpa says every man should own a porch to sit on to watch the sun set in the evening. He truly believe that. So much that he worked for the white folks who use to own Jones Property for four years for free until they gave him the deed. The only money Grandma and Grandpa had while they worked off the deed money was the extra money Grandma made for cleaning for the white folks who lived on Rehobeth Road back then. Them white folks long gone now, except Mr. Bay. Uncle Buddy said, "The only reason Mr. Bay is still sitting around with his nose in the air on Rehobeth Road is because he got one foot on a banana peeling and the other one in the graveyard. And he ain't got nowhere else to go. Period!" Uncle Buddy insists when he's raising hell about white folks.

I'm sitting here thinking about Grandpa and his land; just dreaming about the day I will own land up North.

"Child, what in the world are you daydreaming about now?"

Grandma's always interrupting my dreams just like that daughter of hers.

"I was just thinking about a lot of grown-up stuff."

"Grown-up stuff. Child, you only twelve."

"Twelve-year-olds worry too."

She still asking me questions, when she ain't told me what's really wrong with Grandpa and why she didn't go with him to town.

I guess I'm looking at her cross-eyed or something, because I believe she getting ready to tell me.

"I know you're worried about your granddaddy, but he is fine. He just under the weather, and I thought it would be good for Mer to go with him to Dr. Franklin's so that she can read the medicine bottle he will give your grandpa."

Grandma nor Grandpa can neither read nor write. They both sign their names with an "X" when they have to sign important papers or go into town to buy something on credit. Credit they rarely use. They don't need no credit when my grandpa got money hidden where God can't find it. Now Grandma can count her money. When I go with her to Mr. Wilson's grocery store on Saturday, she always let me count her money after she finishes.

Just to make sure he don't cheat her. Grandma don't trust no white folks. Now that's something she and Uncle Buddy do agree on.

I sit there and listen to Grandma as she gives me every reason in the world that she didn't want to go with Grandpa to the doctor.

"I need to be here picking my strawberries."

"It's just too hot."

"I'm tired this morning."

"Mer can read the medicine bottle."

I just listen as my grandma goes on and on. But Uncle Buddy says Grandpa is never taking her to Dr. Franklin's again, because she cursed that white man like nobody's business when he didn't help him thirty-five years ago. Grandma is still madder at them white folks than Grandpa. Grandpa said she even swore she would kill him and Sheriff Franklin if they ever stepped on Jones Property again. Uncle Buddy said she didn't tell them over the phone because Grandma and Grandpa don't have one. Yes sir, she walked all the way into town and got in their white faces. "Step one foot on Jones Property and I'll kill you both and go to jail for the next of my life." They never did.

Uncle Buddy says Grandma has cursed out more white folks in Rich Square than any colored person alive has and lived to tell it. But I'm not going to tell Grandma I know about her swearing, because I know that that's grown folks business too. If I mention it, she's going to give me one saucerful of coffee instead of two. With my mouth shut, she fills my saucer so full I can no longer see the white ladies dancing in the bottom of it.

We sit there like two grown-ups, not one, until we are finished our breakfast. Grandma gets up and heads for the strawberry patch and leaves me in the kitchen to do the dishes, of course. Sometimes I feel like the only reason I was born into this world is to wash dishes, pick cucumbers, and chop. Uncle Buddy said that it is all post slaves stuff that I am doing around home and on Jones Property. He's right. If I didn't think I would get caught I would put my gloves on that Uncle Buddy gave me to protect my hands from this water.

I have two pairs of dish water gloves. One pair I keep hidden here and the other pair I keep under my bed mattress at the slave house. He said, "Don't let your hands get old before you do. Men look at your hands first, child." One by one, I dip the dancing white ladies into the washtub on the oven. I don't know where Grandma got these plates. Ma said she believe some of them rich folks that use to live on Rehobeth Road gave them to Grandma when she worked for them. They are mighty nice. I am not about to drop one like I did the last time I was here. If I break something I don't get a special treat from Grandma when I finish the dishes. Even at twelve, I still enjoy Grandma giving me a slice of her orange candy after I finish my chores. Ma said I'm too old for special treats. Under my breath, I say that's my special treat from my grandma. Besides, Grandma ain't too good with expressing herself and I know that is her way of saying, "I love you." A person ain't never too old for love.

3

The Strawberry Patch

Grandma is already in the strawberry patch when I get there. I take the shortest row and start picking my own basket of strawberries. Whatever I pick, they are mine to sell at the market. I try to pick a lot except what I don't eat. Every time Grandma looks towards Rehobeth Road to see if Mr. Charlie is coming, I take a bite of the biggest strawberry in my basket. For hours, we pick strawberries and pull weeds without saying a word. Grandma never talks when she's upset. "Just look at her," Uncle Buddy says, and he's right—ain't nothing wrong with Grandma. She can pick ten strawberries to my every one.

I am relieved when I see Mr. Charlie's car coming down Rehobeth Road. I drop my basket and run off to meet them. Grandma don't move. She is just standing there like she was waiting on the Lord. When I get to the Chevy, running as fast as my bare feet can carry me, I don't even stop for the dust to settle around the car the way I usually do. I have to see my grandpa's face. See what them white folks done to him. I open Grandpa's door and God he looks worse than he did this morning. I knew it! I knew it! They done poisoned Grandpa. He looks so pale and tired as Mr. Charlie helps him out of the car. We walk slowly to the edge of the steps that Grandpa built with his hands before they had wrinkles. Ma follows us as I hold Grandpa's hand without saying a word. Not a word does anyone say until Mr. Charlie sets Grandpa on the side of the iron bed with a picture of Jesus hanging over it. Grandpa's overalls touch the pink and white bedsheet hard, like a duck splashing in water. The frame rocks back and front as Grandpa lets out a sigh. "Ay, Lordie."

Grandma comes in through the back door and

she looks worried. "Here, Braxton. Drink this water." Poor Grandpa can barely get the mason jar up to his mouth. Grandma holds it as I watch the frog in his throat go up and down.

I want to ask why he is so weak, but I know that's definitely a grown folks question, so I say nothing. Ma give me the look. The one she gives me when she wants me to leave the room. I let go of Grandpa's hand and go into the kitchen and close the door that I lean on before it closes. Then I take me a mason jar and put one end to my ear and the other end to the door. Just the way Uncle Buddy taught me. Now Grandma uses her mason jars for canning and drinking. Me, I use them to ease drop. No one is going to tell me why Grandpa look worse now than he did this morning, so I have no choice but to use my all-purpose mason jar.

"Mer, what did the doctor say?" Grandma asks in a rare soft voice.

I don't know why she is asking Ma, because when Grandpa left home he could speak for himself. Ma don't answer for a minute. Then all these big ugly words come flying out of her mouth.

"Dr. Franklin says Poppa needs to go to the hospital. He said he might have some kind of brain tumor."

"Lord have mercy! Lord have mercy!"

Grandma just saying it over and over again.

"Don't worry, Ma Babe, I made an appointment for Poppa and we are going to Rocky Mount to the hospital for tests on Monday."

Grandma rarely cries, but she is crying now.

"Shouldn't we take him today? He looks really bad."

"No, we can't take him today. The doctor gave him some medicine for pain and it's making him sleepy. He said he should rest this weekend. Two days of waiting won't kill him."

I can't believe Ma used the word "kill" when Grandpa looks half dead. I just want to run in that bedroom and stick this dirty dishrag that's lying on Grandma's new table in her mouth.

Ma once again has figured me out, because the next thing I know I am looking at Ma's flowered underwear after falling on the floor in front of her. She pulled the door open without me even hearing her come near, and down I fall. No one laughs and Ma doesn't even fuss. She just helps me up and rubs my head. She knows I was only listening because I love my grandpa so much.

"Go and finish the strawberries, child, your grandpa is going to be all right."

I get up with my pride in my pocket, next to my letter from BarJean, and walk closer to Grandpa. I'm not leaving this room until Grandpa gives me a kiss and he knows that. He waves his hand for me to come closer and I almost run. His kiss is so warm, just like I always remember it to be.

Mr. Charlie pats me on the head and Grandma pulls my braids. Ma just looking at me like I ain't walking fast enough. I go outside and stand at the window outside of the bedroom to make sure he is all right. After they pull the covers over Grandpa's shoulders and leave the room, I run to the strawberry patch. This time I move over one row to a longer one. The row that Grandpa always picks from. It makes me feel closer to him.

4

The Walk

The afternoon goes by fast as we pick strawberries and Grandma and Ma talk in codes about Grandpa. That's fine with me. Because Uncle Buddy already taught me to listen in code.

"You know, Mer, I was thinking while you-all were in town."

"Thinking about what, Ma Babe?"

"Well, I reckon I'm going to take your Cousin Irene up on her offer to have a telephone put in the house."

"Really? That's a surprise."

Our Cousin Irene, my aunt Rosie's gal, who lives

in Newark, New Jersey, has tried for years to have Grandpa and Grandma put a telephone in. Grandpa said, "Fine," but Grandma didn't want one. She said she don't want to talk to nobody that don't live on Rehobeth Road. She just stands at the end of the road and yell over to Miss Doleebuck. Miss Doleebuck stands on her porch and yells back. They do that mess all day long.

"Nothing but someone to worry me to death," Grandma declared the last time Irene mention the telephone man coming out.

"I was thinking that Braxton ain't well and if anything happened to him late at night, Lord knows I ain't able to walk to Doleebuck's for help. Even when I get there, they don't have a phone either."

"A telephone is a fine idea, Ma Babe. I will write Irene tonight and tell her. I'm sure she will send the money right away."

I don't have any idea why Grandma can't just go in the jar and take out the money she need for the telephone instead of Irene sending it. Then again, I do know. Uncle Buddy said, "Grandma is a spoil little somebody."

I'm not even trying to pretend I'm not listening at this point.

A telephone on Rehobeth Road. I just can't imagine that. I will tell Uncle Buddy this news when we are going into town tonight, and I can't wait to write and tell BarJean. She will pass the word on to Coy. Just think, I will be able to call her sometimes. I wonder what our number will be.

Only the fact that it is quitting time is getting my mind off of this telephone business.

"It's five, Ma."

"Okay, Pattie Mae, you can stop now."

She never questions me about the time, even if I have never owned a watch in my life. I just follow the sun with my body just like Grandpa taught me. If you can touch the head of your shadow with your foot, it's high noon. If you look straight up at the sun without bending your neck, it's 5 o'clock.

There!

On the nose 5 o'clock.

"Can I check on Grandpa?"

"Yes, but if he is sleeping, don't wake him up."

"All right, Ma." I put my strawberries in the

basket under the shed that my grandpa built and go to check on him.

That should be at least a dollar's worth of strawberries, I think as I wrap them in a cooling sack so the ants can't eat them.

When I look in on Grandpa, he is sitting up in bed. Hudson is up too.

"Grandpa, you're up?"

"Yes, gal, I am. Now come on over here and lend me your shoulder. I want to get out of this bed and take a walk."

"I don't know about this, Grandpa. Ma will be mad."

"I'm her daddy, she ain't my mama. Now stand straight."

Grandpa put both his hands on my shoulders and before I know it he is standing up. Somehow he has managed to put his overall back on over his short-sleeved checker shirt that he said is his favorite. He takes small steps as we walk across the floor like two rats trying not to be heard. Before we make it to the door, Grandma is back in the house, through the kitchen, into the bedroom.

"Braxton Jones, you best get back in that bed!"

Grandpa don't say a word. He just looks at Grandma and she moves faster than I knew she could. I want to laugh, but over her shoulder stands Ma giving me the "You have done it now" look.

"Leave her alone, Mer. I want to go for a walk and she is going with me."

No one argues with my grandpa when he's mad, not even the controlling women. We walk out that door like we have won a war. Hobo stands at the bottom of the steps, wagging his tail like he has won too. He barks once and follows us on our evening walk with his enemy, Hudson. I think he and Hudson even smile at each other for the first time. We get as far as Mer's tree when Grandpa wants to stop and rest.

"Are you okay, Grandpa?"

"I'm fine. Let's sit a minute."

I help him to the ground. Hudson jumps in his lap and Hobo jumps on my lap. The evening sun is not as hot as it was when we were picking strawberries earlier. But it is hot enough to dry the land for chopping on Monday. I don't even want to think about chopping right now. I just want to enjoy my special time with Grandpa.

I sit beside him and close my eyes. I wish that he will be well when I open them.

He is smiling at me when I open my eyes.

"Daydreaming again?"

"Yes sir, I guess I am. I can't help it. I feel like I can make anything happen in my dreams, Grandpa. Anything."

"Like what, child?"

"Well, I can dream about you being well, like you used to be. I can dream about going North."

"Now, going North is something to dream about. But dreaming about me, child, ain't nothing but a waste of time. See, if don't nothing else catch up with you, time will."

Now, I'm not sure what he means by that, but I think it has something to do with dying. I don't know why old folks talk about dying so much anyway. They talk about dying like they are sure they going to heaven. I mean, they say stuff like, "When they carry me to Chapel Hill, I'll get some rest then." They don't mean for church services, they mean for their funeral. I have never seen anything like it in my life. If I want to rest, I don't want to die; I want to go to bed.

So I just change the subject when they talk about dying this and dying that. It's just too much for my twelve-year-old heart to take.

"Would you like me to read you the letter I got from BarJean?" I ask to get away from time catching up with him.

"Go ahead."

I read Grandpa my letter, and we laugh about Coy getting married. So much for keeping secrets. We sit there and watch the sun. It changes its position from 5:30 to 6:00 in silence.

The peace.

The quiet.

But that is short lived.

"Braxton Jones, you and Pattie Mae best come in this house and eat supper."

All the way across Jones Property, Grandma yells.

"She's controlling us again, ain't she, Grandpa?"

"Yep, I'm afraid so. Help me up, child, before she come out here at us."

"I'll help, too," Uncle Buddy says.

We look up and it is my uncle all covered with sawdust.

"Hey, Uncle Buddy, you off earlier."

"I sure am. I got me a date with my niece today."

"Give us a hand, boy," Grandpa says with authority as he reaches up and grabs Uncle Buddy's hand.

We both help Grandpa up. Clearing his throat, he leans against Uncle Buddy for support. Then he stands at the fence that divides Jones Property from Mr. Bay's dairy farm, like he wants to change something in his life. He wants to say something, but he is thinking first. Uncle Buddy is always in a hurry, except around Grandpa. He just stands there and let Grandpa take his time. One day I asked him why he has so much patience with Grandpa and no one else.

"You should always listen to your grandpa. He ain't got no schooling, he just know what he know. Besides, the young are strong, but the old know the way."

That was my moment to ask the big question.

"What about Grandma? She is old and you don't listen to her."

"That's because she's a woman."

I think that makes Uncle Buddy that word I heard Mrs. Wilson at the grocery store call Mr. Wilson—"male chauvinist pig." I looked up the word "chauvinist" in the dictionary. After I read my Webster Dictionary, I knew Mrs. Wilson was right about that husband of hers. And the meaning fit Uncle Buddy, too.

Stroking my hair, Grandpa asks me the questions he has been asking me as long as I've been old enough to listen.

"You see that tree, gal?"

"Yes, sir, I see it."

"From the tree to this fence is Jones Property. I bought it from Wynter Waters, a grandson of a slave owner. Well, I didn't really buy it. I worked for it. Four long years. Not a dime did he give me for my labor for four years. His daddy owned my daddy and his granddaddy owned my granddaddy. I sharecropped free for Wynter until he got tired of farming and moved up North. He said he traded this land for my labor because slavery shamed him. I don't know how true that might be. I reckon he made the trade because no one else wanted to buy land on Rehobeth Road. Whatever his reason was, this is Jones Property now. And it belongs to your ma, Buddy, and their sisters, Louise and Rosie. One day it will belong to you.

"That means you will have a home right here on Rehobeth Road for as long as you live. No matter what you do in life, remember you got Jones blood and a place to call home. Can't nobody take that away from you, nobody."

Uncle Buddy stands there with us and smiles as Grandpa tells us the same story that he tells us at least once a month. I don't mind listening, but I never plan to live on Rehobeth Road after I'm eighteen. But I always let Grandpa have his say. Me, I'm going to get me a train ticket up in Rocky Mount and I will be on my way North forever. Just imagine me living in New York. In Harlem. I hope it is as beautiful as it has been in my dreams.

5

Catfish Friday

We always have Friday night supper on Jones Property. Uncle Buddy don't even stop at the slave house to clean up. He comes straight to the dinner table from the sawmill. Grandma fuss about that sawdust falling everywhere, but Uncle Buddy comes anyway. Catfish, potato salad, green beans, and strawberries for dessert.

Grandma even puts flowers from the flower garden on the table. Yellow daisies in the summer, pansies in the winter. It's so nice. Today Grandma is so happy about her new table, she even goes into the cupboard and put the yellow vase Coy brought

her from Harlem on the table. But I'm not inter-
ested in food, tables, or fancy flowers today. I just
want to eat and get dressed.

"Slow down, child, that food ain't going nowhere."

Slow down. She must be kidding.

Lord, if I could just talk back to grown folks. If I
could, I'd tell her that I have been waiting five
years to go to the movie house. I better not say a
word. I'm going to finish this food and get out of
this kitchen.

After putting my last strawberry in my mouth, I
look at Ma.

"Can I be excused to get dressed?"

"Excused? Girl, you got dishes to wash."

Grandpa quickly comes to my aid. "Let the child
go now. You can do the dishes."

Ma don't like it, but she always gives in to
Grandpa.

"Go on, girl, and you best behave tonight."

Uncle Buddy look at me and winks his eye and I
wink back, just like he taught me when I was eight.

Ma has her way of still babying me. When I get
to my sleeping room, I notice Ma has filled the big

washtub up with water, so I would take a full bath, not just wash up. Lord knows I need to, after no bath this morning. Ma even left some of her powder out for me. I feel like a big girl for the first time.

After I finish dressing, I walk to the front porch where I hear Mr. Charlie, Grandpa, and Uncle Buddy talking. That's where they always talk after catfish supper on Friday nights.

Don't know if they plan to or not, but they sit in the same spot every Friday night. Grandpa in the green rocking chair, with Hudson in his lap, Mr. Charlie in the chair that doesn't rock, and Uncle Buddy on the doorstep. If the ladies come out, those controlling women go in the screened-in porch where the mosquitoes can't get them. I hope they stay inside tonight so Ma won't see my shoes.

"Where is Pattie Mae?" Grandpa jokingly asks Uncle Buddy.

"Don't know," Uncle Buddy says, laughing.

"It's me, Grandpa! Stop playing."

They get a kick out of seeing me all dressed up just to go to the movie house. Uncle Buddy doesn't look bad himself. He has walked back to the slave house and changed into his Sunday go to meeting white shirt and black pants.

"I have the prettiest date in Rich Square. Actually I have two dates."

I don't say anything, because that's grown folks business. But Uncle Buddy is bringing someone with us. I thought it was going to be just us two.

Better not say anything, because Ma will just make me march right back in the house and no picture show.

"Well, let's go, pretty lady."

He don't have to tell me twice. I kiss Grandpa and Mr. Charlie good-bye, and arm in arm we walk across the grass on Jones Property, as the crickets get louder. They are singing like they are cheering for me.

The lightning bugs are everywhere, like they know it's a special night. Hobo is not barking or wagging his tail. He's mad because he ain't going.

"Good night," Mr. Charlie and Grandpa yell across the hot summer air.

Ma and Grandma peep from the window and

wave. They join the men folks in teasing me. Ma claps and Grandma does, too. Then Ma yells, "Nice shoes, Pattie Mae." Thank God she is going to let me live.

Uncle Buddy even opens Mr. Charlie's car door for me. They trade cars on Friday night, so that Uncle Buddy won't have to drive his pickup into town. Mr. Charlie says that boy ain't going to never find a wife driving that truck on courting nights. Besides, it smells like sawdust no matter how many times you wash it. Just as long as it's clean on the inside. "Never mind the smell, it's clean," Uncle Buddy always says. He also swears he will never buy another city car. That's the one thing about Uncle Buddy that ain't citified. He says he don't want one down here in these sticks. Ma told me that one evening about a month after Uncle Buddy got here, he got off work and someone had peed all over his blue Cadillac and broke all the windows out. Ma said it was definitely jealous white folks. But Uncle Buddy ain't never told me nothing about that mess. It took every colored man that worked in town to keep Uncle Buddy from looking for the men who took a leak on his car. He got rid of it so he wouldn't kill no white folks. Ma said that big mess scared her to death. She also said it was grown folks business and she only told me about it because she got tired of me asking what happen to the blue Cadillac Uncle Buddy rode down here from Harlem. After she told me that little bit, she never breathed a word about it. It don't matter to me what we ride in tonight. There is nothing I enjoy more than time alone with my uncle Buddy. Well, maybe being with my grandpa. But my time with Uncle Buddy is so special because he never treats me like a two-year-old. I can ask him anything.

"Uncle Buddy, do you think I will ever get to leave here?"

"Sure you will, gal. Why you think you wouldn't?"

"Well being that I'm the youngest and BarJean and Coy already gone North it seems like it's my job to stay here and help Ma."

"Help Mer do what? Your ma can take care of herself. Besides, she might not say it, but she wants you to get away from here and make something of yourself."

do?" I asks.

cle Buddy laughs as we turn onto t.

Yes, she does. Now, Miss Pattie Mae, do yc want some ice cream?"

"Yes, sir. That would be nice."

I can see the movie house on the next street as Uncle Buddy pulls up to Leon's Ice Cream Shop. I wave at my friend Daniel from school who is crossing Main Street with his ma, Miss Novella.

They wave back and keep on walking.

"What flavor ice cream you want?" Uncle Buddy asks as Miss Novella and Daniel go about their business.

"I'll have two scoops of chocolate."

It's okay to ask Uncle Buddy for two scoops of ice cream. If I was with Ma, I would only ask for one scoop to save money.

Uncle Buddy's whole expression changes when he gets ready to close the car door and walk around the back of the building to get our ice cream. He says colored folks up in Harlem never have to buy nothing from the back of the building.

e Buddy looks so hurt.

turns around to see if I am watching. It
ns like some kind of shame come over Uncle
uddy having to walk around back.

"Be back in a minute," he says. His voice is even
different.

I sit there and watch him disappear into the
prejudice evening light. I got that word from Uncle
Buddy last year. I asked him what "prejudice"
means. He said when I'm around Ma it means
when people of different races don't like each
other. When I'm with him it means, "White folks
hate niggers."

Tonight he hates them back. I can tell from the
look on his face.

It doesn't take him long to return.

"Here you go, pretty lady."

"Thank you, Uncle Buddy, and thank you for
bringing me out to town. You know Ma and me
don't get to go much."

"You welcome and the next time we will bring
your ma."

I smile at the thought of Ma sitting in the movie

house. I bet she will get dressed up to the bone that night. She might even wear the ear bobs that Aunt Louise gave her last Christmas.

"You stay here. I'm going to sit over there on the sidewalk so that I can see Nora coming out of the sewing factory. She should be off work by eight and the picture is at eight-thirty. That will give her a chance to grab some ice cream too."

Well, at least I know his date's name now. But I ain't never heard of this Nora person before. Truth be told, I am enjoying my ice cream and being away from the house too much to care who she is. Uncle Buddy walks back towards the ice cream shop and sits down on the sidewalk. I sit in the car and watch the white folks going in the movie house all dressed up. Of course, they use the front door. It's sad to watch the coloreds in the best clothes they have go in the back door to get their tickets, where Uncle Buddy will have to go, too.

He keeps his eyes on the side door of the sewing factory across Main Street where his date will come out of. I guess she's an afternoon cleaning lady there, because Uncle Buddy said all the sewing ladies are poor white trash.

Uncle Buddy speaks to everyone that passes, even the white folks who just nod their heads like the cat got their tongue.

I am looking so hard at the people that the time starts to slip away.

One white lady comes by and stops right in front of Uncle Buddy because he has his feet out on the sidewalk just a little bit. Grandpa done told him a thousand times that he ain't in Harlem and to move off the sidewalk when white folks coming by, to avoid trouble. She doesn't say excuse me or nothing, just looks at Uncle Buddy like he is a dog in her path. Her hair is back in a bun like she wants everybody to get a good look at her prejudice face. If you don't notice her face, you can't miss her ugly orange dress.

Uncle Buddy stands up to let her by.

What is wrong with her? She starts to walk faster, and then, out of nowhere, she let out this loud scream.

"Oh, my goodness!" she yells.

Then she holds her hand to her pale chest like she is having a heart attack.

Uncle Buddy looks around confused as he realizes she is yelling at him.

"Come on, gal," he yells to me.

I jump out of the car and we go to the back door of the movie house, buy our tickets, and go inside.

"Maybe we should go home, Uncle Buddy. That white lady is mad."

"We can't do that, gal. If we do, white folks will think I have done something wrong. Let's go up in this balcony, see the picture, and then we will go home."

"But what about your date?"

"I'll explain to her later."

It taking forever to get to the balcony, where the screen seems so far away.

"Why do we have to sit up here?" I ask.

"The same reason we had to buy our tickets in the back and eat last month's ice cream. We have to sit up here for the same reason that lady yelled like I was trying to hurt her. You can't even look at white folks round here."

That is the last thing Uncle Buddy says before the movie start. He is so mad that I can feel him breathing hard next to me. Uncle Buddy doesn't move all night, not even to get me the popcorn he promised. My first picture show just ain't going well at all. I couldn't tell a soul what this movie is about. I just want to go home where I feel safe. Back to Rehobeth Road. Back to Jones Property. I am glad to see the words "The End" come across the screen.

"Let's go, gal," Uncle Buddy says in a voice I ain't heard before. A scary voice. A real scary voice.

Holding my hand tight, Uncle Buddy and me walk quietly down the steps, through the lobby, and out the back door to Main Street.

"That's him, officer."

The words come out of nowhere.

It is that pale white woman's voice.

The law, Sheriff Franklin, looking old and feeble, is standing at Mr. Charlie's car. So are two other lawmen.

Uncle Buddy looks scared for the first time since I've known him.

The sheriff is taller than Grandpa and as red as the sunset.

"Boy, we need to talk to you."

"My name is Goodwin Bush."

This must be serious because this is the first time I have ever heard Uncle Buddy use his real name.

"Okay, boy, but we still need to talk to you. This lady said she was walking home from the beauty parlor and you made a pass at her. Is that true?"

"No, it ain't. I was just sitting right over there waiting for my friend to get off work. I don't know this lady and I sure ain't tried to harm her."

"Now, you wouldn't be calling a lady a liar, would you?"

"I ain't calling her a liar, but I never touched her."

"Tell it to the judge, nigger!"

Sheriff Franklin is mad. Maybe he is getting revenge for what happened with Grandpa all those years ago. Maybe he knows Uncle Buddy let the air out of his tires. Whatever—we are in trouble.

Everything starts moving faster than the ants in our front yard. Faster than the red ants. The black ants. The fire ants. How am I going to remember what to tell Grandpa? The lawmen pull my hand out from Uncle Buddy's hand that I am holding on to so tightly. The silver handcuffs are around both his wrists now and I am alone.

"What about my niece?"

"We will take her home, but she is the least of your concerns, boy."

Sheriff Franklin leads Uncle Buddy to the backseat of his car and the second lawman leads me to the other car. The third lawman grabs Uncle Buddy's keys and get behind the wheel of Mr. Charlie's car to drive it home.

Uncle Buddy does manage to yell, "Take my niece to my daddy's house."

I watch as the sheriff drives away with Uncle Buddy and drive in the opposite direction with me and Mr. Charlie's car. At least they aren't keeping Mr. Charlie's car. I cry harder than I did at my cousin June Bug's funeral as they disappear with Uncle Buddy. All the way home, I picture them beating up my uncle Buddy, like they do in the cowboy pictures. It's so dark. I can't even see the cotton.

When we get to the house, I am wet all the way to my panties with tears and sweat. The lawman drives up to Jones Property blowing his horn. When he sees Ma run outside, he gets his white behind out and lets me out of the backseat. He had me locked in like I am a prisoner.

Ma screaming like a crazy person.

"Lord, child, what happen? Where's Buddy?"

I can't get a word out. I fall on Ma's arms like a newborn hungry baby.

Ma turns to the lawman.

"Where is my brother?"

He just looks at her like she is a piece of dirt.

"Jail."

With that one word, he and the other lawman drive off and leave us standing there.

Weak, Grandpa makes his way on the back porch and so does Grandma. Mr. Charlie, who is still there, follows them onto the porch. Grandpa unlocks his smokehouse door and pulls out his rifle. Miss Doleebuck came over while I was away, and she comes out behind Mr. Charlie.

"Where's my boy, Pattie Mae?"

"They took him to jail, Grandpa, and he didn't do nothing wrong."

"Get your gun, Charlie."

Mr. Charlie asks no questions. He gets his cane and goes in the trunk of his car. His shotgun is longer than Grandpa's is.

Grandma and Miss Doleebuck go into their control mood.

Grandma speaks first.

"Put them guns away right now. Braxton Jones, you know you ain't well and Charlie, you ain't used a gun since the months before Sunday. Who you going to shoot? The law?"

No one moves. Grandma speaks again.

"Now, Mer, you go over to Mr. Bay's and give him a quarter to use the phone. Call the law and find out what they charged my boy with."

"But, Ma Babe."

"Don't Ma Babe me, gal! Go on!"

It is like Ma is five again. She is walking across Rehobeth Road to Mr. Bay's, mad as she can be. I know Ma don't want to go. She hates asking Mr. Bay for anything. But she will do anything for her Buddy. Grandma looks at me and reaches out for my hand.

"Come in the house, child. This will pass."

She nods for everyone else to follow her. Mr. Charlie and Grandpa walk slowly behind the women folks. They talk low. The only word I can hear good is "Masons." The men folks on Rehobeth Road don't talk much about their organization. I don't know how you become a member, but I know Grandpa and Mr. Charlie go to meeting once a month and they never let the women folks hear anything about what they are doing.

Don't let a Mason die! Them Masons come from everywhere to a Mason's funeral. And they don't let nobody carry the body of a Mason that ain't a Mason. I've only been to one Masons' funeral. That was June Bug's daddy, Uncle Pete, who died the year before June Bug drowned. The Masons might have been sad, but Aunt Rosie wasn't. They were divorced and she said, "Peace go with him and joy behind him."

The grown folks take their places on the front porch. I run to the kitchen to get a mason jar to ease drop.

Ma is back in ten minutes from Mr. Bay's house

and the grown folks' talk begins as I go to my room with my jar. Yes, we are spending another night on Jones Property. Ma tells them, "Ain't nothing we can do until Monday morning when the courthouse opens."

My body will not stay awake, not even to ease drop. Our catfish Friday done turned to a nightmare. I put my jar under the bed. They talk. I sleep.

6

The Queen's Chair

I'm not sure if anyone is getting any sleep tonight other than Grandma and me. She says the Lord is going to take care of this, and she gets up Saturday morning singing and getting ready to go to town. Grandpa says we should all stay home. But Grandma keeps on dressing and tells me to do the same.

Not even Uncle Buddy's troubles will stop Grandma from her Saturday ritual because somehow over the years, Grandma has managed to control Mr. Wilson, too. I think going in his store, bossing them white folks around, feels like justice to my grandma. Justice for all the colored folks who don't have the courage to do what she does every Saturday morning.

Mr. Charlie comes for us at 10:00 just like he always does.

"Good mornin', Mr. Charlie."

"Good mornin', Pattie. Good mornin', Babe."

"Mornin', Charlie," Grandma says, like it hurts her to talk.

I help Grandma in the front seat of the car and close the door gently. I climb into the back right behind Mr. Charlie, so that we can talk. But he is too upset about Uncle Buddy to talk and he hardly says a word all the way to town.

It's really not far to Wilson's Grocery in the heart of Main Street. But it always takes Mr. Charlie about twenty minutes every Saturday morning because he drives, as he puts it, at his own speed.

The slower he drives, the sadder I become as I look out at cotton and the coloreds chopping it even on a Saturday morning. Then I remember what Grandpa told me last year when I was complaining about fieldwork. "Don't let nothing that you can change worry you." I know in my twelve-year-old heart that I will soon be leaving Rehobeth Road and the cotton fields forever, so no need to worry. But what about Uncle Buddy? We can't change what's happening to him. He's just sitting in that jail. He don't belong in no jail.

When we get to Wilson's Grocery, I open the door to the store for Grandma, and to my surprise, Mr. Wilson has already put a chair in the middle of the floor for Grandma to sit in. Usually, she will pull her own chair away from the table where the white men sit to play chess and talk all day. Mr. Wilson seems to really like Grandma and he lets her come in and rearrange his chairs every week. Uncle Buddy said all them white men are doing is sitting round that table calling us niggers. I told Uncle Buddy that I think Mr. Wilson really like Grandma, but he said Mr. Wilson don't like nothing black, he just know that her bra is filled with green. Grandma walks over to that chair and sits down like she is a queen. Mr. Charlie comes in to buy some tobacco. He looks at her and shakes his head. "I'll be back in two hours," Mr. Charlie announces, biting into a fresh piece of tobacco.

I know he will have Miss Doleebuck with him when he gets back. He rarely drives the two controlling women to town together. He says they talk too much and try to tell him how to drive when they are together. I have taken that ride with him many Saturday mornings and he ain't lying about them trying to tell him where to turn, how fast to go, and when to stop. It's a mess. I'm telling you. It's a mess.

The minute Mr. Charlie walks out the door, Mr. Wilson come over with his first samples of meat for Grandma to pick from. She ain't about to walk around the store like other customers. Mr. Wilson rolls back the wax paper enough for Grandma to see his prize meat.

"How do you like this piece of fatback, Miss Babe?" he ask, pointing at the biggest piece. She is shopping for meat for her and Ma. Ma tells her every week not to bring her nothing but chicken, but Grandma always add another meat using her bra money for Ma and me.

Grandma studies all three pieces of fatback like

they are paintings in the state museum that our class went to last year up in Raleigh.

"I don't know, Wilson. Let's see what else you got." That's the way Grandma address all white folks, by their last name, with no Mr. or Mrs. She says if white folks can't call colored folks by their name with a handle on it, she ain't calling them Mr. or Mrs. And she says she ain't calling them their first name either, because she don't want them to think she's their friend.

Mr. Wilson turns red as a beet and walks back behind the counter where Mrs. Wilson is standing, so he can pick some new fatback. Mrs. Wilson waves and rolls her eyes at the same time. Grandma never even acknowledges that woman. She says, "Mrs. Wilson's mouth just as good as mine. I don't understand head and hand movements. If she can't speak, I can't speak."

Mr. Wilson ignores both of them and comes back armed with three new pieces of fatback laid out on wax paper.

I think Grandma just like making that white man walk back and forth.

"Take your pick and I will wrap it up for you."

Grandma still ain't sure, but she knows she has less than two hours to buy her goods. Mr. Charlie surely will be back on time with the other controlling woman.

"That first piece you show me will do fine."

Mr. Wilson goes behind the counter to wrap the fatback. I see him weighing the meat. I look hard because Grandma told me to keep an eye on him to make sure he don't cheat on the scales. Again, she don't trust no white folks. When he comes back, he has pork chops, ribs, you name it. But I've seen this parade so many times, I just walk over to look at the map on the wall.

Don't know where Mr. Wilson got this map, but it has been my underground railroad since I was tall enough to stand on my tiptoes and see it. The world outside of Rehobeth Road. I have been trying to leave Rehobeth Road ever since the traveling salesman came with the encyclopedias that has every state in it. I was five or six when the white man in the black car came with the books he was selling in the backseat. He said Ma didn't have to pay the whole amount that day. He gave the books to her on time. That's what folks on Rehobeth Road call credit—time. So within minutes we had new red encyclopedias and I started to read about all fifty states. Mainly New York and New Jersey, because that's where all the folks from Rehobeth Road go when they leave here. New York looks so far away on the map. Farther than in my dreams. Five states away—Virginia, Maryland, Pennsylvania, and then New Jersey. I touch the map in the spot that says New York. I usually point it out to Uncle Buddy every Saturday. Everything feels wrong today. Wrong because I usually wait for Uncle Buddy to look at the map with me, so that he can point out all the places on the map that he traveled while working in difference factories up North.

I walk outside and sit on the steps. The sawmill across the road looks so ugly to me. I bet nobody there is going to stick up for my uncle. Now he's just three doors down, in the jailhouse. Three doors down! I have to see him. My feet feel so heavy as I try to walk down there to get a peep at him. But I walk on. The windows are high and I can't see inside. I walk around back where the windows are covered with bars. This must be where they are keeping him. I move closer.

"Uncle Buddy."

No answer.

"Uncle Buddy."

Two hands appear at the barred window.

"Pattie Mae, is that you?"

"Yes, sir, it's me. Are you okay?"

"I'm fine, gal. Now get away from here."

"But I want to see you."

"No! Now go on! Tell everyone I'm okay. Now get!"

My heart feels like snow in July.

"Bye, Uncle Buddy."

"Bye, baby."

His hands disappear into the dark hole behind the bars.

I start to walk away, but then I hear a voice. A voice that ain't Uncle Buddy. A woman's voice. But who? I go back to the corner of the jailhouse and peep to see who has come to see Uncle Buddy. I can't see her face good, but I don't think I have ever seen her before. This strange lady takes an old wooden soda crate and puts it under the window. She stands on it so she can talk to Uncle Buddy through the bars.

Her voice is soft and citified like Aunt Rosie.

"Is a man named Goodwin Bush in there?"

Uncle Buddy comes back to the window.

"Ain't nobody in here but me, Nora."

So that's Nora. She reaches her hand through the bars and touches Uncle Buddy's face.

"Buddy, are you all right?"

"I'm fine *now*, sugar. But you can't stay here."

"I know, but I had to come to see you."

"Now, Nora, you know what they saying about me ain't true, don't you?"

"I know and don't you dare try to explain nothing these country-ass white folks done to you."

"I will be out of here soon. Don't worry."

I can't see Uncle Buddy well; I can just see his hands touching Miss Nora's face. She doesn't say a word as she reaches in the bars farther and touches his face. Uncle Buddy's hands leave her face and rub her neck. I don't think I am suppose to see all of this, but my feet are stuck. My eyes are too. His big hands make their way down her neck to her blouse and before I know it Uncle Buddy is rubbing her right tiddie like he is a baby trying to get some milk. I think this feels good to her, because she is making funny faces and some strange noise. I wonder if she going to get worms for messing with Uncle Buddy. Because Uncle Buddy is the one who said boys give girls worms. This is too much. It is definitely time to get back to the store. Now, that's some *real* grown folks business.

I walk back to the store so fast after seeing Uncle Buddy. I want to feel sorry for my uncle Buddy, but judging from the noises he and Miss Nora making, he doesn't sound too sad to me. When I get to the grocery store door, I peep in past the soda machine so that I can see Grandma. She is almost finished with her Saturday ritual. I say nothing about talking to Uncle Buddy. And I shoo ain't going to tell her I saw Uncle Buddy give that woman the worms. Then the moment arrives that I understand why Mr. Wilson put Grandma's chair out for her.

"Miss Babe," he says slowly, like he know the question he is about to ask is none of his business. "What's going on with that Buddy Bush mess?"

"Mess?" Grandma snaps back. She is mad.

Grandma says white folks are always asking coloreds questions, but we can't ask them anything. "Don't even know where most of them live unless you they maid," she says.

"It ain't no mess! My boy ain't done nothing wrong." Grandma turns away from Mr. Wilson and puts her right hand deep into her green and white dress. Down to her bra where the money is. In that sock is more money than I knew one woman could put in her bra.

"How much I owe you today?"

Mr. Wilson knows Grandma is mad.

"That'd be twenty-nine dollars and eighty-two cents."

She counts out exactly $29.82.

Then Grandma turns to me.

"Count it again, Pattie Mae."

I count it again.

$29.82

I hand her the money back.

She gives it to Mr. Wilson, who is two steps from getting a Babe Jones cursing.

Then she gives him a "Don't ask me nothing else about my boy" look, and says, "Good day."

Grandma don't like the fact that word has already got around in Rich Square that they have arrested Uncle Buddy. I swear I see smoke coming from under her coattail when she stands up. Coattail is what the women on Rehobeth Road call their dresses. Now, why can't they just call a dress a dress? She never looks at them white folks as she walks out the door and leaves the queen's chair in its place. I believe this is what Uncle Buddy meant when he said, "A lady always knows when to leave a room."

"White folks tell all of colored folks' business!" Grandma says loud enough for Mr. Wilson to hear as she slams the door in his face.

I want to tell Grandma that I just read that the NAACP is calling coloreds Negroes now. But she ain't going to listen. She says I'm not old enough to tell her nothing but the time. If she only knew what I just saw back at the jailhouse, maybe I can get some respect around here. I have just seen some real grown folks' mess. I sure did.

I don't say a word as we get into Mr. Charlie's car after Mr. Wilson load our six bags. Four for Grandma and Grandpa and two for Ma and me. Grandma and I climb in and Miss Doleebuck climbs out of the backseat. Miss Doleebuck never rides in the front seat because she says she feels better in the back. That means she doesn't think Mr. Charlie is a good driver. Mr. Charlie tells Grandpa and me that he doesn't care where she sits as long as she doesn't open her mouth. Not one word.

Miss Doleebuck is dressed like she is going to church. If she is going to Jones Property, she dresses the same way. Always in a nice dress with a hat. In the summer, her hats have fresh flowers from her garden on them. In the winter, they have all kinds of berries on them. Her hats are mighty pretty on her long white braids and her tan skin.

Uncle Buddy told me she got Indian blood. Grandma found out that he told me that mess and she told him to shut up talking about what kind of blood Miss Doleebuck got.

"Good-bye, Miss Doleebuck," I yell from the backseat.

"Good-bye, grandbaby," she yells back as she kisses Grandma like she always does. If these two women see each other ten times a day, they kiss and hug. Just kiss, kiss, hug, and hug.

Mr. Charlie waves to his controlling wife and Miss Doleebuck marches into the store to terrorize poor Mr. Wilson some more.

Grandma hardly murmurs a word all the way home. She is still mad at Mr. Wilson for getting in colored folks' business and Mr. Charlie knows something has happened. But he ain't paying one bit of attention to her silence as he singing his favorite song. I join in with him as he sings "Amazing Grace" loud enough not to hear Grandma huffing and puffing. I make up my mind at this moment that as soon as I am old enough I am going to learn to huff and puff, too. Not only that, I am going to get my driver's license so that I can drive myself to town. I bet Grandpa and Mr. Charlie will think I'm controlling, too, when I have my driver's license. I look out the window and sing louder.

Just think, when I'm riding to New York I will see lots of cars and highway, not cotton and field workers.

I sing louder and don't look at Grandma who is trying to give me the "Shut up" look through the rearview mirror. I'm not going to look. I'm not going to look at her. She wants to control me, just like Mr. Charlie and Grandpa were talking about on the front porch last week.

I only look in the front seat long enough to see Mr. Charlie laughing to himself at Grandma in her control mood. The truth is, she is mad and she is worried about Grandpa and Uncle Buddy. She is ready to get home.

"Drive a little faster, Charlie."

"Now, Babe, you just sit tight. We will be home soon."

Poor Mr. Charlie speeds up and as soon as we

turn on Rehobeth Road, a stray dog is running towards the car. Lord, we miss that poor dog by an inch. Mr. Charlie hits his brakes, causing Grandma to grab the dashboard with one hand and somehow reach into the backseat to hold me down with the other hand.

"Hold on, Babe," Mr. Charlie sings in the same breath with "How sweet the sound."

They both singing "Lord, have mercy!" at the same time. I can't say a word. I'm just glad to be alive.

"Slow this car down, Charlie!" Grandma yells.

I want to scream, "You just told him to drive fast!" But I don't have to. Mr. Charlie beats me to it.

"Now you want me to slow down. I don't know why you and Doleebuck don't get license of your own and stop telling me how to drive."

All the way home they argue. I close my eyes and think about my train trip. I think about never chopping again, about Grandpa feeling better, and Uncle Buddy coming home.

7

What a Time

When we get home, no one even mentions Uncle Buddy, and I don't tell a soul that I went by the jailhouse. The thing I know now, that I didn't know when I left Jones Property this morning, is that grown folks can get worms, too. Whatever worms are!

I'm telling you, ain't nobody saying a word on Jones Property.

Everyone is waiting for Monday morning to come, like them white folks are going to grow a heart between now and then.

Grandma finally breaks the silence.

"Mer, you and Pattie Mae need to stay here until this mess with Buddy is cleared up. White folks crazy when they mad. They might come by y'all house and try to harm you."

I hope they burn the whole house down while we here. That way we can stay on Jones Property forever.

"You believe we in danger, Ma Babe?"

"I don't know. Just stay here till things look better."

Ma never argues with Grandma. She puts her last biscuit in the pan and sticks it in the oven. Wiping the flour off her hands, Ma looks worried.

Grandma goes about her daily chores as Ma gathers her two grocery bags for her walk home.

"Pattie Mae, stay here with your grandfolks. I will be back soon. I will bring your clothes for church tomorrow. And something for you to wear in the field next week."

Just what I need, my field clothes.

But staying here is just fine with me. A Saturday night with Grandpa.

As soon as I can't see Ma anymore, and

Grandma goes into the sitting room to dust, I go in to check on Grandpa, but he is taking a nap. Sitting here watching him seem like forever. His light skin is starting to look like the rattlesnake that he killed last year in the strawberry patch. Why does he look so old? Then I just close my eyes and pray, but not aloud.

"Oh, Lord, please help my grandpa. I promised Grandpa I was going to Shaw University someday. He promised me he would come to my graduation. He always keeps his promises, so please let him live until then. Pleeeease. Grandpa is a good man. And Lord, while I'm praying, please, please take care of my uncle Buddy. Amen."

After I finish begging the Lord, I climb over Grandpa's weak body and lie down beside him. The cotton sheets are wet on his side of the bed. It's June, but not hot enough for all that sweat. I don't say anything. I just lie there and listen to him breathing.

It's getting late now and Ma still ain't back. Grandma's walking through the house, closing all the windows. With her fly shot, she spraying bug spray in each room until every bug, ant, and candle fly in the house is dead or dying. Hudson sees her coming and he runs under the bed. Surely Grandpa and me will die in our sleep with no way to breathe.

I don't care. I keep my eyes closed and think about how unbearable life will be on Rehobeth Road if something bad happen to Grandpa. Then I start thinking about us dying together. Grandpa and me in heaven. What a time we would have away from the controlling women.

I fall to sleep and dream about heaven. No snakes, no mean sheriff, no cotton to chop. Uncle Buddy is in heaven with us, not in jail. It is so beautiful.

8

The Amen Corner

Grandma is up praising the Lord this Sunday morning. She cooks and prays. She asks the Lord to heal Grandpa and to bring Uncle Buddy home. She speaks in tongues every time she prays about Uncle Buddy. Ma joins her and they shout all over that kitchen, before and after breakfast.

When Mr. Charlie arrives, Miss Doleebuck doesn't stay sitting in the car like most Sundays. She comes inside, lays her hat on the table, and grabs Grandma's hand and they pray again. Then they shout together. One by one, all dressed in black, in the middle of June, the women march out to the car. Grandpa and me follow them in shock. Mr. Charlie loses his patience with the women folks halfway down Rehobeth Road. "Can y'all please wait until we get to church before you do all this carrying on?" Grandma stops shouting long enough to roll her eyes at Mr. Charlie and then shouts louder. I want to laugh so bad I don't know what to do. I can tell by the carrying on that the women folks are doing that there is going to be some shouting going on in Chapel Hill Baptist Church this morning.

"Amazing Grace," "Precious Lord," "Somewhere Around God's Throne"—all before we reach the church parking lot.

When we get there, the women folks are out of breath and I am scared to get out of the car. I just don't know what they are going to do next. I look at the tree and the poles and they are all filled with signs. Me and Ma are the only two in the car that can read and today I wish I couldn't read either. I make the mistake of reading one of the signs aloud. "Look at the signs, Grandpa. They say 'Free Buddy Bush.'"

Right there on the church ground the women shout.

Lord do they shout.

Once inside the church it is chockablock full.

Reverend Wiggins is preaching like he ain't never preached before. He mentions Uncle Buddy in every breath and the church is on fire with the spirit. All the deacons stomp their feet louder than usual in the amen corner to the right. The deaconesses in the amen corner to the left shout amen and fan each other with the new church fans. Miss Sally faint while Betty Lou sing "Let the Church Say Amen."

"Go on and preach," Miss Lucy Bell yells as she grabs her wig so that it won't come off. Then she dances down the aisle to her own beat. When the choir sing "Take Me to the Water," she joins their beat and her wig is now flying across the red carpet, under the wooden bench, where I am sitting next to Grandpa.

When it is prayer time, Ma and three other women, including Miss Doleebuck, almost faint at the altar. Brother Boone even takes his green necktie off. Mr. Charlie just nods his head to agree with "the word," and pats Grandpa on the back every time he thinks he is getting upset. I'm holding Grandpa's hand tight and I pray this service is over soon.

By two o'clock, the women of the church have shouted more than I have ever seen them carry on before. Surely Sheriff Franklin will hear them a mile away. He is probably ready to release Uncle Buddy now so he can be saved from hell, that everyone here have condemned him to.

Lord, when service is over I am so tired. So is everyone else. I just pray that Sheriff Franklin releases Uncle Buddy by next week's service. I can't go through this two Sundays in a row.

9

Pretty Lady

*I*t's Monday morning, the land is dry, and I have to go back to the cotton fields to chop weeds. Ma tells me that what was going on with Uncle Buddy is grown folks business and no harm is going to come to me.

I wave good-bye to Ma and stand at the end of the path and wait for the truck to pick us up. Jones Property is before the slave house if you coming from the other end of Rehobeth Road near the river, so Randy can see me standing here. He is the official driver for Ole Man Taylor this summer.

The Edwards are already on the back of the

truck, all ten of them. Randy's sisters and brothers. Like me, they don't have a daddy either. They live in Old Man Taylor's other house on Rehobeth Road with their ma, Miss Blanche. When I climb on the back of the truck, I notice a new woman with us. She is sitting in the front with Randy. She can't be his girlfriend. Randy is Miss Blanche's middle boy, but he ain't old enough for a girlfriend. I believe he is about sixteen. He shoo ain't old enough to be driving. But Ole Man Taylor don't care as long as we get to the field every day. I try to get a good look at her, but that is not going to happen with the Edwards blocking the window like sardines in a can.

I touch my friend Chick-A-Boo, Randy's youngest sister, on the shoulder. "Who's the new lady in the inside of the truck?"

Chick-A-Boo is mad about her being in the inside. "She is some city lady named Nora and she thinks she is too light skinned and pretty to sit back here with us. She came back to Rich Square a while ago and according to Ma, she went to work at the sewing factory Saturday morning and they told her she didn't work there no more. So I guess she going to have to get off her high horse now, working with us in the fields."

"Nora! That's Uncle Buddy's friend."

"We all know that," Chick-A-Boo snaps. "That's the reason she got fired."

I'm not about to tell Chick-A-Boo that I saw Uncle Buddy give Miss Nora worms, because she is still fussing about Miss Nora riding in the front with Randy. I didn't get a good look at her face on Saturday because I was so busy looking at Uncle Buddy's hand on her tiddies.

Finally I said, "Don't worry. When she finishes chopping and pulling weeds, she will be black like the rest of us." I try to assure Chick-A-Boo. But no one is as black as Chick-A-Boo, who we called "Skillet." Now, Uncle Buddy calls her "Pretty Lady."

Uncle Buddy says it must be a dead cat on the line, because Chick-A-Boo is the only dark Edward. On Rehobeth Road "dead cat on the line" means you don't have the same daddy that your sisters and brothers do. Ma told Uncle Buddy he don't know who that girl daddy is and he best stop talking to me about Miss Blanche's business. And she says it don't matter what color you are if you that pretty. As a matter of fact, she said it don't ever matter to God what color you are, just to the crazy folks around here. And everybody says Chick-A-Boo is the prettiest girl on Rehobeth Road. Maybe in all of Rich Square. Right now she's just being jealous. So I'm not going to pay her any attention while she talks about Miss Nora. She know better than to talk about folks anyway. When she does, I tell her she sounds like Sylvia. A nasty two-faced little gossip. I tell her that Grandpa says, "Never worry about the bone, just the dog that's carrying it."

When the truck turns onto the dirt path, all I can see is cotton plants with weeds that don't suppose to be in them, all mixed in together, waiting for us to chop out. Our hoes lie at the end of field where Randy left them last Thursday, before the big rain came.

When the truck stops, I jump off first, trying to get a better look at Miss Nora. Everyone runs to the field, trying to get the row that has less weeds and grass on it. I don't budge. I want to see the city lady. I saw that mess she was doing with Uncle Buddy, but never did see her face. I wonder where her worms are. What is she like, the one Uncle Buddy likes enough to take to the picture show? Why would she give up the city life to come back to Rich Square? I will ask her sooner or later. What about the movie theaters and all the stores I see on Grandpa's TV? Don't she want to go to the Chinese restaurant on Saturday nights and the Savoy? I hear that they dance all night there.

When she steps out of the truck, I want to laugh. But Grandma and Ma would skin me alive for laughing at anyone. I want to laugh because I had never seen anyone dressed up going to chop cotton before. Miss Nora has on a pair of pretty blue pants with little splits on the side. Her blouse is red with white flowers on it. Her shoes are a dead giveaway that she hasn't been in a field in a long time, if ever. They look almost as good as Ma's Sunday go to meeting shoes, just lower heels.

I move closer, so I can speak to this city lady.

"Hey, Miss Nora, my name is Pattie Mae."

"Hi, Pattie Mae. How are you?"

"Kind of sad about my uncle Buddy, but I'm okay."

"Me too, but he's going to be all right. You must be Mer's girl."

She pauses. "And Buddy's niece."

"Yes, ma'am, I am."

"Your Uncle Buddy told me all about you, and you look just like Mer when she was a young girl."

"You know my ma, too?"

"Yes, Lord. She was the smartest thing at Creecy School. I used to cheat off of her paper every day."

Miss Nora laughs at her own self.

I laugh too because everyone is always talking about how smart Ma was in school and how they all used to cheat off of her papers. One day Uncle Buddy was copying Ma's work so hard that Ma said he wrote her name down instead of his own. He got ten licks for cheating and Ma got one lick for not telling the teacher.

Folks say the only reason Ma didn't finish school and become a schoolteacher is because when Grandpa bought his land on Rehobeth Road, there was no school bus to pick up the colored children that far away from town. My uncle Buddy, who had quit school years earlier, wouldn't get out of bed and take Ma to school, so she eventually quit. Too far to walk. I guess he was a little lazy back then, but not now. Not my uncle Buddy. Everyone in Rich Square said Ma would have surely become a schoolteacher if she had just been able to get to the schoolhouse. Grandpa wouldn't take her because he ain't drove one mile since he got hit over the head. I don't mean to be selfish, but I'm kind of happy Uncle Buddy slept late back then. If Ma had become a schoolteacher, I don't think she would have had time to have babies and I would have never made it to the oven. Schooling or no schooling, Miss Nora, like everybody else around here, knows that Ma ain't no dummy. When folks tell Ma she smart, she always say, "I ain't smart, I just know what I know."

"So where's Mer?" Miss Nora asks.

"She can't make it. Grandpa, he's not feeling so good, and she and Mr. Charlie taking him over to Rocky Mount to the doctor today. Then she is going to go and talk to the law about Uncle Buddy."

Miss Nora looks sad.

"Tell Mer hello and tell her that I hope Mr. Braxton will feel better soon."

I assure Nora I will tell Ma that she asked about her as we walk to the cotton field together. Everyone else has already started. Randy walks between four rows of cotton so that he can chop two on each side of his.

He chops fast.

"Such a smart boy," Ma always say when she talks about Randy.

To me, if he is so smart, he should know he don't have to chop four rows at a time. He still ain't going to get but $2.00 a day. The same amount I'm going to get for taking my time.

Miss Nora reaches in her pockets and pulls out a pair of white gloves nice enough to wear to church. She slowly put them on as I watch in amazement. I know when I get to Harlem, I will learn to put my gloves on just as easy. The only difference is, I'm not coming back here to chop in my gloves.

I wish for gloves when I pick up the raggedy hoe

that has been left behind for me to use. Then I wish I was back at Grandma and Grandpa's house. I wish I could make him feel better. But most of all, I wish Uncle Buddy was home.

At least I have someone to talk to, because Miss Nora chops even slower than I do. Unlike everyone else, who is now all over the field chopping fast, like they are going to make more money if they finish earlier. The way I see it, we are all going to make the same pennies. No need to hurry.

The morning is going by fast, as I question Miss Nora about the North. How many stoplights are on her street? We only have one light in Rich Square. Where does she shop? I want to know everything.

Miss Nora just smiles and talks. She seems happy to tell me all about the big city. I can tell she loves the city life. So why did she leave? I just have to find out. But I know that's grown folks business like everything else on Rehobeth Road except the weather and the time.

I want to drop my hoe and run over there and shake her back to her senses and say, "Get out of here while you can, lady! If you stay, you will chop all summer, pick cotton all fall, and carry wood until March, maybe April, of next year."

Instead, I watch her carefully pull up the weeds and lay them down like they are babies. I want to yell again, "Just throw the damn thing on the ground, please." Better not do that, either. Ma would kill me for cursing. Finally, I get up the nerve to ask Miss Nora about my uncle.

"Miss Nora, can I ask you a grown folks question?"

"What is it, child?"

"How did you meet my uncle Buddy?"

"How did I meet him? I don't ever remember *not* knowing Buddy. I grew up right here on Rehobeth Road, too. Buddy was my boyfriend in high school. He just up and left for Harlem one day and the next year I followed him there. Of course, Buddy had a new girl by the time I got there. But he never did marry. Me, I eventually married someone else."

"Well, why did you two come back here? Ain't nothing here."

Miss Nora is looking at me like Grandpa does when I have said something stupid.

"Honey," she says, "it's always something at home. I just came back a few months ago after my divorce was final. Buddy never told me why he came back. But I am glad. Your uncle ain't lost his charm one bit. We just started going to the movies together on Friday nights about two month ago. I feel so guilty about what happen to him."

I can't believe this woman is feeling sorry for Uncle Buddy after he done gave her the worms. I better try to comfort her.

"Don't feel guilty, you didn't do nothing wrong."

She still loves my uncle after all these years. Maybe that's what Grandpa meant when he said, "Better the devil you know than the devil you don't know."

Miss Nora says nothing.

I say nothing.

Instead, she is sad and so am I, as we both think about Uncle Buddy.

I check the time with my foot. Grandpa said you ain't a real farm girl if you don't know how to tell time with your foot. I have no plans of being a farm girl for long, but this telling time thing comes in handy. Uncle Buddy don't like it when I do this. But he can solve that and buy me a watch. Ma says, "Don't be begging your uncle." Watch or no watch, he don't think I'm going to be a good city girl if I don't break my country ways. But I know I will be, one day. I move my foot to the head of my shadow.

There it is, right on the nose. It's lunchtime.

"Miss Nora, it's twelve noon. We can stop for lunch now."

Miss Nora looks at me and smiles, like she knows my little secret way of telling the time.

Everyone rushes to the old oak tree to have lunch. When I get there, all the Edward children have beaten me to the best shade spots. They sit together and laugh at Randy's jokes. I usually sit with Chick-A-Boo, but not today. Today I am going to sit right here with Miss Nora. If I sit close enough, I will probably see the worms.

Miss Blanche cooked her children two chickens, some bread to share, and she froze them some Kool-Aid, that I plan to ask for a glass of later. Ma never froze me Kool-Aid, just iced tea. She told me that tea is cheaper and Miss Blanche know good and well she can't afford no Kool-Aid. Sometimes Randy will trade me Kool-Aid for tea, if I ask him.

My little lunch bag with my name on it is lying on the table that Randy put here every morning. It's his job to put our lunch bags out at 11:50. If he put it out too early, the ants will eat and we go hungry.

Miss Nora didn't bring a lunch bag. Just an apple rolled up in a napkin and some water that she left on the dashboard of the truck. I hope that Chick-A-Boo doesn't see her get her apple out of the truck. That will really push Pretty Lady over the edge. Because she want Miss Nora to eat pork and beans just like we are eating. Miss Nora told me why she's only eating an apple and drinking water. She's on a diet. Now that's big stuff in Rich Square. A person on a diet.

She bites her apple slowly and don't drink all of her water at one time, the way most grown folks do around here.

We only have thirty minutes for lunch. That is just enough time for me to eat my pork chop from last night's dinner and my can of beans.

Ma's leftover salad would spoil before I could eat it, so pork and beans with pork chops is my lunch.

When we finish lunch, everyone takes their positions back in the field where they have left their hoes and hats. Our straw hats are all different colors, like we are in a fashion show. Every summer, when chopping time is over, I bury my hat on Jones Property. Not that I want a new one next year. I just never want to see this one again. I take my hat to Jones Property to put pie on Ole Man Taylor's face. He can't hear me, but it's my way of saying, "Take your hat. Take your land. My grandpa got his own land." Then I give that stinking straw hat a funeral. Me, Hobo, and Hudson. This year, I think I will burn them, hat, hoe, and all, the morning I leave for Harlem.

Burying just isn't permanent enough. Last year I buried the ugly shoes that Ma had bought me at the thrift store over in Jackson. I carried them in my lunch bag to Grandpa's and buried them at the far end of Jones Property where no one ever walks.

Ma was looking for Hobo one day after I had buried the shoes, and there they were. A big rain had washed those ugly shoes up and I had to wear them to school until they were too small. Ma said, "I hope you have learned a lesson." I definitely had. Burning is better than burying. Uncle Buddy laughed at me for a month. He said, "Now Pattie Mae, never try to outfox the fox. Mer is a fox." I wish he were here with me now to laugh. To do anything.

After lunch, it seems like the day is going by so fast. I am glad because I want to get home, change clothes, and find out if there is any news about Uncle Buddy and Grandpa's condition. I bet he will feel better after the doctor gives him something to throw up all those roots Grandma has put in his stomach over the last fifty years. That's how long they've been married. That's how long she's been trying to control my grandpa.

Ma told me to get off the truck at the slave house so that we can get more clothes. Last to pick up, first to get off the slave truck. After I get my envelope from Randy with eight dollars in it for the last week's pay, I run down the long path to our house. Friday is usually payday, but we didn't work Friday because of the big rain, so we get our money today. And I would have gotten ten dollars if we had worked on Friday.

"Good-bye, everybody. Good-bye, Miss Nora." Pretty Lady is rolling her eyes at me just because I'm waving good-bye to Miss Nora. But I'm not thinking about Chick-A-Boo with her spoiled self.

10

Cloud Heads

Ma is in the slave house kitchen. But I know something is wrong the minute I walk near the stove because ain't no supper on it. Ma always have supper ready when I am done chopping. She never chops until 6 o'clock with us. At 4:30 each day, Randy have to bring her home. If he is not there, Ma will just walk. No matter how far, Ma just walks.

"Evening, Ma."

"Evening, child. How's your day?"

I don't know why Ma asks me that. My day was terrible out there in that hot damn sun from sunrise to sunset. I don't say a word, but Ma can tell I am cursing to myself.

She finally say, "We took your grandpa to the doctor today."

"I know. Is he okay?"

"No, Grandpa ain't okay. The doctor says he got some kind of brain tumor, just like Dr. Franklin said. They say he too old for them to operate on him and sooner than later he will go blind."

I want to scream, but nothing will come out. I just can't imagine Grandpa not being able to see me. What if he can't see Grandma's strawberry patch no more, his rocking chair, Mr. Charlie, Jones Property? He has to see Uncle Buddy get his freedom back. I wonder if Grandpa is going blind because Sheriff Franklin hit him on his head all them years ago. If I learn that to be so, when Uncle Buddy gets out of jail we will go out there and flatten some more tires.

I try so hard not to cry. Please, Jesus, I don't want my grandpa to go blind.

"What about Uncle Buddy, Ma? Is he coming home today?"

"No, child. Uncle Buddy ain't coming home today. His trial been set for the thirtieth of June. But Poppa going to try to get him out on bail next week. He just ain't feeling well enough today. And the law wouldn't talk to him right now anyway."

"What about Uncle Buddy's job?"

"He don't have a job no more. The sawmill fired him. Mr. Quick came by Jones Property today while we were in Rocky Mount. He told Ma Babe that Bro can't work there no more."

I'm not asking another question, because Ma's tone is saying that she has said all she is going to say. She has three tones and I know them all well. Tone one is Ma is in a good mood, we can talk about anything. Tone two is a serious tone, and don't mess with me. Her third tone is so sad that it always makes me sad.

Knowing she's in her third tone, I do my chores without saying one word. First, I bring the clean clothes in off the clothesline in the backyard. Then I pump some water and pour it on the flowers around the doorstep. No need to pump water for supper, since Ma says we will be leaving soon for

Jones Property. I bring the ax inside and put it behind the kitchen door as tears roll down my face. I can't help thinking about Grandpa and his ax that he brings in every night from the woodpile on Jones Property. He told me, "Ain't no need to lock the door if you leave the ax outside." I asked him what that meant. Two things, he said. One, someone can break in your house. The other meaning is don't trust nobody with your business. I think about all the things he has taught me as I finish my chores.

Every time I do my chores, I think about that song that Miss Annie Bell sings on fourth Sundays. The words go like this: "One of these days and it won't be long, you will look for me and I will be gone." Now, she is singing about going to heaven. Well, I ain't ready to die and I don't want Grandpa to die, but I am ready to get out of this slave house and go North.

When I finish my slaving, we gather our pillow slips filled with clothes for a week and start our walk to stay on Jones Property. Ma carries the big pillow slip of clothes and I carry the little one. She is real quiet until she looks up at the heavens.

"It's surely going to storm tonight, Pattie Mae. Just look at the cloud heads."

Sometimes I almost forget that Ma is a little girl at heart. She's Grandpa's little girl, his baby girl. And she has never forgotten all the things they used to do when she was little. Like looking up at the sky and finding different-shaped clouds that look like different animals. Grandpa taught her and she taught me. Now Uncle Buddy can pick cloud heads too, but he says that it's countrified so he hardly does it. When he does pick them, he always find people up there, not animals. He showed me one that looked like Deacon Smith one time when they were mad at each other about parking spaces on the church ground. I think I will just stick to animals so that Ma will not tear my tail up again for doing disrespectful mess.

"Look at that one, Ma. It looks like a cow."

Ma joins me in my search for cloud heads.

"That one looks like an angel," she says and actually smiles.

"Do you believe in angels, Ma?"

"Of course I do and you should, too."

"I do, Ma, and I believe they are watching over Grandpa and Uncle Buddy right now."

"Shoo they are, child. They looking over all of us."

We pick cloud heads all the way as we walk down Rehobeth Road. When we get to Mr. Bay's dairy, I start to walk fast trying to avoid the bulls.

"Slow down, girl."

"But what about the bulls?"

"Can't go through life being scared of anything, girl, not even a bull."

Ma smiles and walks slower. Then she opens her top so that the bulls can see her red T-shirt. She looks at those bulls like "I can wear red whenever I want to." I feel so safe with Ma, safe on our way to Grandma and Grandpa's. Safe on Jones Property. The place Grandpa said will always be my home.

11

Yellow

Grandma's rooster that I named Felix wakes me up at 5:30. He and Grandpa don't let 5:31 come around and their eyes still closed. Can't believe Ma let me oversleep. On chopping days, I have to be up at 5:15, not a minute later. I ease out of bed and into the hallway. Grown folks are talking on the front porch. Everyone is there: Grandma, Grandpa, Ma, Mr. Charlie, and Miss Doleebuck. They are out there having a grown folks meeting.

Grandpa, as sick as he is, he is definitely in charge. See, when Grandpa calls a grown folks meeting, even the controlling women stop all their mess.

"We won't be able to see the bail bondsman until sometime next week. They been putting me off all week. Mer says that ten percent of the two-thousand-dollar bond is two hundred dollars. Is that right, Mer?"

"Yes, Poppa, that's right. You got enough money buried under the house to pay it. Or you can use the house for collateral and you wouldn't have to use your cash."

"What's collateral?" Grandpa asks.

"That's when you use your land or house as money to secure something. If that person jumps bail, the law will own the land and the house."

Grandma don't seem too pleased with that idea. So she adds her say. "We will use the cash. White folks will never own Jones Property again. Not as long as me and Braxton got blood running through our veins."

Grandpa agrees.

"So, it's settled. We will go to town with cash and speak with the law. Mer, tonight when the sun go down, you need to go under the house and get the jar."

"Yes, Poppa."

They always wait until dark to go under the house. They act like we got a neighbor to see them or something. Ain't nobody next door on either side and don't nobody else know it's under there. Mr. Bay don't look over here during the day. He shoo ain't going to look over here at night.

See, ease dropping really pays off. Now I know what is going on. Next week, they will get my uncle out on bail and he can stay home with us until the trial.

I am so glad when Miss Doleebuck asks what are the charges.

"Braxton, I don't understand what they say he did."

"Attempted rape," Mr. Charlie says.

Grandpa adds, "Not just attempted rape, but attempting to rape a white woman."

Miss Doleebuck is as confused as I am.

"Talking to a white woman don't mean he tried to rape her," she finally says.

Grandpa goes on to explain the rest. "You don't understand white folks, honey. As soon as the law started to talk to that white woman, she started crying and said that Uncle Buddy tried to rape her around the building earlier in the evening."

I can't believe it. He didn't do nothing to that pale white woman.

Grandma speaks up when she can see Grandpa is getting mad as two roosters fighting. "I'm worried about that boy," she says. "He may never make it to trial. They just as soon kill him in that jail cell as they would a dog."

Oh, God, they can't kill Uncle Buddy for something he didn't do. I have to tell them what I saw.

Forgetting that I am in my nightgown, I run out on the porch.

"Grandpa, it's not true, it's not true. I saw the whole thing."

"Child, what did I tell you about listening to grown folks talk?"

Even with her brother's life on the line, Ma still teaching me good manners.

"I know, Ma, but I have to tell the truth."

Grandpa is not in the mood for Ma being in control.

He is giving her the "Shut your mouth" look and she finally shuts up.

"Pattie Mae, go and get dressed. Then you can come back and tell us again what you saw," Grandpa says.

I was wondering when they were going to ask me again. They ain't asked me a word since I came home screaming Saturday night.

This morning is one of the longest mornings of my life. I tell what I had seen that night one hundred times. When Randy comes to pick me up for chopping, Ma waves for him to go on to the field without me.

After the grown folks listening to me over and over, Grandpa takes me in the sitting room and says tell him one more time. I try to remember everything that happened. Even what kind of ice cream Uncle Buddy had. Vanilla.

"Pattie Mae, your grandpa is proud of you."

That makes me feel so good. Good to know that I am helping my uncle.

Good to know I am helping Grandpa.

Then he walks out the house, off of Jones Property over to Mr. Bay's, and does something he never does: He ask to use the phone. Grandpa calls the law and tells them to come hear what I have to say.

They never come. We wait all day. All the next day. We wait a whole week, but they still do not show up. Whatever I had to say, I will have to say it at the bail hearing is what Sheriff Franklin sends word by Ole Man Taylor to tell Randy and Randy tells Grandpa. Grandpa calls the sheriff again when he gets that news. Then Sheriff Franklin tells Grandpa not to bring me after all, because I am too young to go on the stand. That ain't even no law, I don't think. Just something white folks made up to keep Uncle Buddy in jail. Grandpa hangs up Mr. Bay's phone and swears he is not calling back.

"I'll see them in the courthouse," he murmurs, as he is giving Mr. Bay another quarter.

I hold Grandpa's hand tight as we walk slowly away from Mr. Bay's phone and back home.

That is the last quarter Mr. Bay ever got from us.

Come this morning, while Uncle Buddy is sitting there waiting for Grandpa to make his bail, the phone truck drives up.

Here it comes.

It's yellow.

I am summoned by Ma to stay home with her so I get to witness my grandfolks get their own phone. The first colored folks on Rehobeth Road to get a phone.

The white man who is here to install the phone barely speaks.

"Mornin', sir. I guess you here to put our phone in?" Grandpa asks.

Sick or not, Grandpa wants him to hurry up so that they can go and bail Uncle Buddy out of jail. It has taken ten days for the judge to agree to see Grandpa.

The phone man nods his head and comes inside. He has a black box with him, a rope, and some other stuff in a big bag. Surely this will take all day. Grandpa can't stay here and watch this historic event, so I'm going to keep an eye on the white man until Grandpa gets back. I also want to be here when the phone rings for the first time, and so do most folks on Rehobeth Road.

Mr. Charlie drives up to get Grandpa as folks gather in the yard.

"Bye, Grandpa. Bye, Mr. Charlie. When y'all get back we will have a telephone." They laugh at me and wave good-bye.

Most folks didn't go to the fields today. A lot of white folks told field folks to stay home today, fearing trouble. If they don't let Uncle Buddy out on bail, there just might be trouble on Rehobeth Road. So they are all here to see the phone man. Everybody knows we are getting a telephone because I told Chick-A-Boo, she told Randy, Randy told Miss Blanche, and the rest is history. She told everybody. Miss Blanche is a nice lady and she can sing like an angel. She likes to talk, but only about good stuff. She is always proud when coloreds do well, so I know she couldn't wait to tell all of Rehobeth Road about the new phone.

Folks are here like we are holding the state fair in the yard.

Grandma is not going to let all these folks in the

house. Nobody but Miss Doleebuck, who just walked in the door. Everybody else is just standing around in the yard, looking at the truck, looking at the back door, waiting for the white man who is giving us a connection to the world to come out.

They know they will not have to ask Mr. Bay to use his telephone again in life. He has made his last colored quarter. Grandma told me last night that she will only charge a nickel, if it ain't long distance.

The time is moving so slow. So slow that the morning glories are starting to go back into hiding and the dew is drying up. Grandma pays us no mind as she and Ma go around back to pick more strawberries.

I carry water out to the folks waiting. They talk about everything, but mainly they talk about Uncle Buddy. Word has gotten around that Grandpa is going to try to get Uncle Buddy out today, and folks are whispering that Uncle Buddy ain't hardly getting no bail.

The phone rings for the first time.

It is the telephone man testing the line.

I realize that this is the first time in my twelve years on this earth that I have ever heard a telephone ring, except on Grandma's TV. Everyone in the yard fall silent like they are in prayer meeting. The telephone man's job is done and we now have life to the outside world. Life without paying a quarter.

After the white man finishes loading his equipment in the back of the truck, he leaves without even looking into the face of one colored person. I hate to leave all the people who have come over for the excitement, but I have to go inside to see our new telephone.

When everybody starts to leave, I wave good-bye and almost run into the house.

The telephone is yellow. Yellow just like the white man's truck. I walk over to the coffee table in the living room to get a better look. It's ringing. Lord have mercy.

It's still ringing. Who would be calling us already?

I pick up our telephone for the first time.

"Hello, Jones residence." I say it just like the white women on TV.

"Hello, this is Mrs. Margaret Anderson, with Carolina Telephone Company, just checking the phone line."

"I think it is working fine," I announce like an adult.

"Okay miss, welcome to Carolina Telephone Company."

"Thank you," I answer like I had ordered the phone service myself.

Just as I am hanging up, Grandma and Ma come in the sitting room. Ma is mad at me for answering that telephone and you know what? I don't care. When I touch this phone, I feel good.

"Pattie Mae, this is not our telephone. Why are you answering it?"

Grandma saves me.

"Honey, she can answer it every time it rings for all I care. I ain't too crazy about having no phone. It ain't nothing but something to worry me to death."

"All right, if it's okay with Ma Babe, it will be your job to answer the phone when we are here. But if any white folks call about Bro, don't tell them nothing."

I am happy to hear her say that, but I wonder when we are going home. If I'm assigned to the phone, that means we are staying here a little longer. Maybe we are never going back to the slave house. Never! I don't want to go back. Grandma and Grandpa has everything that we don't have. A water pump on the back porch—ours is in the yard. They have lots of new stuff that Grandpa is buying each month with the money from selling the lumber. But no matter how poor we get, Ma don't ask them for nothing. She told me, "We ain't asking for nothing. My poppa and Ma Babe worked for their stuff and it's theirs and nobody else's."

But Grandpa is always trying to share with us the nice things they buy. What he don't buy, he builds with his own hands. Grandpa's even built a indoor bathroom; now all he has to do is figure out the plumbing. Surely, as soon as he is feeling better, he will figure that out too. I sit at the telephone table that he built two years ago.

I sit there waiting and wondering. Every few minutes, I peep through the window to see if Grandpa and Mr. Charlie are coming. Will

Grandpa like the new phone? Will he have Uncle Buddy with him when he comes back? Is Grandpa going to be okay?

Just when it's time to worry some more, I look down Rehobeth Road and Mr. Charlie's car is coming at five miles per hour.

"Ma, hurry! It's Grandpa and Mr. Charlie. Uncle Buddy ain't with them."

We all rush to the door as they pull into the yard.

I can tell that Grandpa don't have good news.

Everybody takes their positions on the front porch. Grandma and Ma go into the screened-in porch and sit in the green swing. Mr. Charlie and Grandpa sit in their usual places.

I say hello to the grown folks and voluntarily go in the house before being ordered to.

The door is open, so I will not need my mason jar today.

Grandpa explain to Grandma why he didn't bring their boy home. "Them white folks are as mad as all getup. They said Uncle Buddy can't have no bail and they said he will have to stay in jail until his trial starts June thirtieth."

Grandma don't say a word for a minute. Then she ask, "Did you see him?"

"I saw him, Babe, and he look like he doing okay."

"Do he look like they feeding him?" Ma asks.

"He do. He looks like he eating just fine."

After that, the grown folks don't say nothing. They just sit there and look at each other until lunchtime. Every now and then Miss Doleebuck starts to sing a church hymn. I think if Grandma try to join in, she will cry a river. I want the court date to hurry up and come, so that Uncle Buddy can leave this town and go back North to enjoy his life.

His life before coming down South. Before taking me to the picture show. Maybe I will go with him up North and never come back. Never!

Everything changes around the house after they refuse Uncle Buddy's bail. I overhear Grandpa tell Mr. Charlie that white folks are up to no good again.

He can just feel it in his bones. White folks are mad about what that white woman told them

Uncle Buddy tried to do to her. She ain't doing nothing but lying. But they believe her. They are talking about a hanging. It's 1947. Surely they can't hang him.

Somehow the word has reached all the way to New York. On Thursday my letter from BarJean is just filled with questions.

Dear Pattie Mae,

How are you-all doing? I am fine. I
talked to Coy and he said that he
heard from one of the guys from Rich
Square that there could be more
trouble at home. Write me back and
tell me what is going on.
   How's Uncle Buddy?
   Please stay close to home and don't
tell anyone except family about what
you saw.
   Also, Irene told me that Grandma
and Grandpa were getting a new
telephone. Do they have it yet? If so
please write me back and give me the
number.

Love, your big sister
BarJean

Dear BarJean:

Yes, we have the telephone. It's yellow! Ma said it is not our phone. She said that it belongs to Grandma and Grandpa. But Grandma said I can answer it all the time, because she really doesn't want a phone anyway. The only reason she got it is so that she can call the doctor if she needs to for Grandpa. Anyway, the number is 919-555-1919. BarJean, Uncle Buddy is okay, but they have accused him of something really bad. It's grown folks talk, so I will let Ma tell you about that. Please pray for him and for Grandpa, who ain't feeling so good.

Love, Pattie Mae

12

The Chain Gang

This morning I wake up to a horrible noise coming from the sitting room.

A man crying.

A woman crying.

No! Two women crying.

What in the world is happening this early in the morning? The rooster ain't even crowed yet. I peep through the keyhole in the sitting room.

Grandpa, Grandma, and Ma are all crying. Somebody must have died during the night. Lord, did them white folks hang Uncle Buddy?

I grab my pink house duster from the bedpost

that faces the window. The window that faces Rehobeth Road.

And that is when I see why they are crying.

I can't believe it. The chain gang is working on Rehobeth Road, paving the road. Is that Uncle Buddy?

Yes, it's him.

Right in front of Jones Property.

In a red and white pinstripe suit with chains around his legs, he is pushing a wheelbarrow with sand in it. Folks have been saying for years that they were going to replace the gravel road with tar—but not with my uncle Buddy's hands.

My feet can't move. Something wet runs down my legs. I pee right there on the floor. Can't control it. Tears from my eyes and the water from my private parts is the last thing on my mind.

I let out a holler that I feel clean to my bones.

Uncle Buddy must hear me hollering because, just for a second, his head raises up in the air like a peacock. Ma surely can hear me, but she is in so much pain, she can't move.

Me, I feel like dying. Heaven or hell will do, I

just want to die. I somehow stop crying long enough to take some dirty clothes out of the hamper and wipe the pee up off the floor. Not feeling or smelling so good, I sit on the floor with no strength to move. All my strength is in the sitting room, crying right along with everyone.

All morning we cry. No one comes to my room and I'm not going in the sitting room. No one fixes breakfast. It is as though the world has stopped. At least it has stopped on Rehobeth Road. Yes, the world has stopped on Jones Property. Only the door divides my pain from their pain.

I guess Mr. Charlie eventually see Uncle Buddy out there in that hot sun, and I can hear him and Miss Doleebuck talking as they coming down the path that leads to the house.

Mr. Charlie is not driving today. Mr. Charlie says when trouble comes, you should walk it to the Lord in prayer.

"Open the door, Braxton. It's me and Doleebuck."

Nobody gets up to let them in, but Mr. Charlie has a key to the house like Grandpa has one to theirs, so he just lets himself in. On my knees, I look through the keyhole at them hugging each other.

Miss Doleebuck starts praying like Uncle Buddy really is dead and that makes Ma cry louder.

"Come on in, Jesus, help us if you please," Miss Doleebuck shouts.

Mr. Charlie takes charge.

"Now, y'all got to pull yourself together. Crying ain't going to make the devil leave here. It ain't going to make them white folks behave. What you going to do is get up from here, get dressed, and go on with your day. We can't let Buddy see us like this. We have to get ourselves together, because we ain't got no other choice. Y'all hear me?"

In between "Lord have mercies," Ma and Grandma say yes. Even Grandpa agrees, and he don't answer to nobody but the Lord.

One by one, we change into some everyday clothes. We know folks will be coming by to see about us once they learn the law has sent Uncle Buddy to the chain gang until his trial. Now folks on Rehobeth Road can be nosy when they want to, but this is different. Folks are some kind of upset about my uncle Buddy. They ain't coming by to get a look at their neighbor in pinstripes. They just coming by to pray and make sure everyone is all right. That's just what folks do for each other on Rehobeth Road. Miss Nora came, but she was crying so bad, she left right away.

Folks just worried to death about us and Uncle Buddy. Blood or not, folks consider Uncle Buddy our family.

Ma don't have to say it: I know I am staying home from the fields today for sure. I have decided to sit on the porch with Grandma all day. She just sitting here in Grandpa's rocking chair, rocking back and forth. Grandpa ain't been out here all day. He is getting sicker by the hour, knowing his boy is out here being treated like a dog. Ma told Grandma the doctor said Grandpa can't be under any stress. None. If this ain't stress, I don't know what is.

It will be lunchtime soon and we still ain't had breakfast. I need to check the time so I step off the porch. Using my bare foot, I touch the shadow of my head.

"Grandma, it's time to eat."

"I ain't hungry."

"But you got to eat."

"Later, child."

But Miss Doleebuck ain't hearing nothing about later. She is in the house cooking fried chicken, mash potatoes, black eye peas, and biscuits. She makes lemonade and lunch is served. She even takes Grandpa his lunch in bed. Ma ain't left Grandpa's side all day and she ordered me not to leave Grandma alone, except to pee. Grandma and Ma have a ladies' agreement. "When the devil comes, you look out for your pappy and I will look out for me." That's what I heard her tell Ma.

Grandma always makes it clear she can take care of Babe Jones. So when trouble comes, Ma goes to Grandpa and Grandma goes to the Lord.

"Here's your lunch, Grandma."

"Thank you, child. Where's your someteat?"

"I'll eat it in a minute."

Grandma takes her plate and I go back inside to get myself something to eat. When I get back on the front porch, she is still sitting there, taking small bites like it is the Last Supper. I sit down beside her and join her in her unspeakable pain.

People continue to come by, but they say little or nothing. They just hug us and pray. Some sit a while and get up and go home. Miss Katie just came in with a cake and Miss Thelma is right behind her with some fried pork chops and some Kool-Aid. I'm telling you, these folks act like Uncle Buddy done died and went to glory. I sure hope Miss Thelma feels sorry enough for us to bring a lemon pie tomorrow. Can't nobody cook lemon pie like Miss Thelma. Some folks even come by on their lunch break from the fields. The few that are still working. Folks just plain scared to work today.

Round six o'clock, the guards round up Uncle Buddy and the other men to go back to the jailhouse and the prison camp. They don't take that gun off of Uncle Buddy the entire time. Like he is going to run with the big chains on his ankles. Then they all get into a bus with bars all around the windows. Grandma puts her head down and only the sound of the bus going down Rehobeth Road, past Jones Property, can be heard. I ain't going to say a word because Grandma's hurt done turn to anger.

Miss Doleebuck is back at the stove and Ma is still sitting with Grandpa. Mr. Charlie sits on the back porch all day. Every now and then he goes in the house and sit with Grandpa. Grandma, as usual, decides it is time to change things around this house.

"The devil is a liar," she says as she stands up and go in the house, slamming the door. Now Grandpa got two screen doors to fix.

"Doleebuck, you and Charlie been here all day," Grandma says. "Now, y'all go on home, I can finish supper. The law got my boy, but they ain't got my soul. We going be all right. That's what the Lord made tomorrows for."

I can smell the corn bread on the porch. Grandma don't need to cook no meat. We're eating Miss Thelma's pork chops tonight.

Miss Doleebuck wipes the corn meal off of her hands and hugs Grandma.

"I reckon we best get on home. It's time for Charlie to take his blood pressure medicine."

They gather their things and say good-bye.

"Bye, Mr. Charlie. Bye, Miss Doleebuck," I

yell as I walk them to the end of the path.

"Bye, grandbaby," they yell back as they cross the road that now has sand on it waiting for gravel. Sand laid by Uncle Buddy's hands.

We go to bed early. We go to bed sad.

This morning I hear Grandma long before 5:00. I get up, too, because I know the chain gang will be back with Uncle Buddy. Sure enough, when they come, Grandma is waiting. She ain't crying this morning. She just sitting in her chair and watching the devils giving Uncle Buddy orders of what to do today. I sit here holding her hand for hours, while the sweat rolls down Uncle Buddy's body. He never looks towards Jones Property. He waves slightly when the guards aren't looking. But he never looks our way. He waves again in the afternoon. But he still don't look our way. He don't want them white folks to see how much they are hurting him. How much they are hurting the only ma my uncle Buddy can remember.

When they leave with my uncle Buddy, Ma starts crying and praying. Grandpa gets out of bed and takes his place on the porch. Mr. Charlie is here now and sits with Grandpa until it gets so dark they can't see each other. This is going to be a long sad night.

Ma comes on the porch and announces that I will be going back to work in the fields tomorrow. She says Randy will look out for me. I don't want to go, but I have to. Ma sent word by Mr. Charlie for Randy to pick me up in the morning.

Randy shows up, all right, but he ain't stopping at the end of the road. He comes in the yard and everyone on that truck gets out and speak to Grandma, who is back in her chair.

"Morning, Miss Babe."

"How you doing, Miss Babe?"

"Can we do something to help, Miss Babe?"

Miss Nora hugs Grandma and me real tight. But she don't say nothing. Not one word. Then she move out the way and all Miss Blanche children hug Grandma.

This goes on for about ten minutes, then we all pile on Ole Man Taylor's truck and go to work.

Miss Nora and me talk all day in the field about

what's going to happen when Uncle Buddy goes to court.

"Miss Nora, do you think they are going to put Uncle Buddy in prison for life with those other men?"

"Now, child, stop worrying about grown folks business."

She may be a city woman, but she still believes that grown folks business is grown folks business. She give me some more information about New York and stops talking about my uncle. I really don't care about the North right now. I just want Grandpa's tumor to go away and Uncle Buddy to come home.

I'm so glad it's Friday, so I can stay home with my folks for two days. We off work at 2:00 today because it is so hot that the sun has made Chick-A-Boo blacker. I see Grandma sitting on the porch long before we make it to Jones Property. Uncle Buddy is still out there in that hot sun working like a dog. I go straight to the front porch.

"How you doing, Grandma?"

She don't even do her control thing; she answers me in seconds.

"Hey, baby, I'm fine. Ole Man Taylor let you off earlier today?"

"Yes, Grandma, he did."

"You wash up and get you someteat."

I do as I am told, and check on Grandpa, who is sleeping. My mind must be playing tricks on me because the sound I suddenly hear coming from the road is women folks singing. I rush to the front door and Lord I am in shock.

Sure enough, it is the women from church. The women from the choir.

All of them.

Walking.

Walking and singing.

"Jesus, what in the world is they doing?" Grandma says as she stands up.

They are all dressed in white and Miss Cora Mae Jones, who ain't related to us, is leading the choir.

"Hush, somebody calling my name," she sing on and on.

By the time they get to the doorstep, Grandma is singing, too. I join in as Grandma shouts for joy.

"Yes, Lord, yes," she says as her apron flops up and down like a rooster's feather.

Now them white folks guarding Uncle Buddy don't know what to do. They just look at us and order the men to keep working.

Grandma yells as loud as she can in between hymns, "The devil is a liar."

I want to yell, "That would be you, white boy!" But they might shoot Uncle Buddy if I do that.

Grandpa somehow makes it to the window and looks. He knows he can't do nothing with the women of the church. Ma is now out here shouting, too.

They are having church right here this afternoon and there is nothing nobody can do to stop them.

I am shouting too, and run to the end of the path in the spirit, to listen to what the white men are saying.

They pay me no mind.

"Let's get them niggers out of here. They all done lost their minds."

They start loading Uncle Buddy and the other men on the truck and it is only 3:30.

"Praise him, oh praise him," Grandma shouts as they leave Rehobeth Road and give us our dignity back.

Ma looks at Grandma, who is still caught in the spirit.

"You think they will be back, Ma Babe?"

"Don't know. But if they do, we will meet them at the gate with Jesus, until they see the glory of the Lord."

We are so tired from shouting we are going to bed earlier again tonight.

I can't wait to get up tomorrow.

I want to see if they are coming back.

5 o'clock. No guards.

6 o'clock. No guards.

When Randy picks me up, it is clear the devils are not coming today.

They have heard the coming of the Lord. Never to return.

13

The Trial

*T*oday is June 30, 1947.

We dressed like we are going to church.

But we ain't.

We going to a trial. Uncle Buddy's trial.

Mr. Charlie picks us up. Grandpa must be losing his sight because Grandma had to help him dress this morning. Nobody says a word all the way to the courthouse.

I've never been in a building this big before. Nor have I ever seen this many white folks in the same place at the same time.

I look in the little box that the jury is sitting in.

That is where the men who will decide about my uncle's life sit.

Uncle Buddy is in trouble, judging by these faces.

"Sit here." Ma points for me to sit where Uncle Buddy can turn around and see me. He does and I feel much better.

It is a long day in that courthouse. They call all the white folks' names who have trials for one thing or another today before they get to Uncle Buddy. When they finally call Uncle Buddy's name, the judge takes a sip of water.

A long sip.

Then he reaches in his pocket and bite a piece of tobacco. Is this what white folks go to law school for? To chew tobacco in public places? In between chews, he say, "This trial has been rescheduled for November 1, 1947."

He takes another bite of tobacco and say, "This court is adjourned."

I don't know what that word means. I turn to Ma.

"Ma, what does 'adjourned' mean?"

"Baby, it means your uncle can't come home."

Ma starts crying, then screaming like Uncle Buddy is dead.

Grandma cries for the first time in weeks and Miss Nora does too. I didn't even know she was in the courtroom until I hear her crying.

Grandpa curses like I have never heard him curse before, and the law leads Uncle Buddy away.

We go home.

No one says a word at dinner. We have been staying here on Jones Property for over a month and it don't look like we are going home anytime soon. I'm not going to ask when. The other day when I asked, Ma just said when things are better. That's definitely not now. Uncle Buddy's in jail and Grandpa says he is in danger, that they want to keep him there long enough to kill him.

It don't take long for word to get around Rehobeth Road that them white folks have no intention of sending Uncle Buddy to the prison in Raleigh.

They are planning something else. Something bad.

The week is going by so slow as Grandpa becomes weaker from his tumor and the pain of

Uncle Buddy being in jail. His sight is worse than yesterday. I can tell because every night before she goes to bed Grandma is laying his clothes out to wear the next day. But he keeps on having them nightly meetings with the Masons. Because Grandpa ain't feeling well, they come to the house and talk to him about something real important and leave.

Come Saturday night, some of the younger men show up and say they have come for Grandpa. I know this is serious, because Grandma ain't even trying to stop him. Plus, Grandpa is dressed like he is going to Chapel Hill. Mr. Bishop leads Grandpa out the door and down the steps.

My grandpa built those steps; now he can hardly see them.

I stand on the porch and watch him go into the unknown with those men.

Colored men who are fed up with white folks about the way they're treating Uncle Buddy.

Rehobeth Road is quiet after they drive away. Except for Hobo barking. Hudson is on the front porch in Grandpa's rocking chair. That cat ain't no fool. I think he knows where Grandpa is going.

I'm trying to sleep, but I can't. Where is Grandpa and what is he doing?

I almost jump out of the bed when I hear a voice at the window calling my name. I peep outside.

It's Randy.

"What are you doing here?"

"Get dressed. We are going into town. There is going to be a mess out there tonight."

"Are you crazy? How are we going to get there?"

"I'm driving Ole Man Taylor's truck."

"Ole Man Taylor? No way! You ain't suppose to drive that truck after chopping hours."

"Come on, chicken! Chick-A-Boo is waiting for us."

If we get caught, Ma is going to kill me. Miss Blanche is going to kill both her children and give them a double funeral like June Bug and Willie's.

"Wait! Let me see what Ma is doing." Thank God, Ma and Grandma are asleep in the sitting room. I ease into the sitting room and they both are fast asleep on the two sofas that line the walls.

I walk back to the window and whisper, "I'll be out in a minute."

Lord, I keep thinking about the whipping I will

get if Ma wake up in the middle of the night and realize that I'm gone. But that's unlikely, because Grandpa says if a train came right down Rehobeth Road, into the sitting room, the controlling women would not move. Nothing wakes them up when they are sleeping after a long day in the strawberry patch. Let's hope that train don't come tonight.

Ole Man Taylor's truck seems bigger than it ever did as we drive away. When we reach Rich Square, Randy parks at the schoolhouse.

"Why are we parking here?"

"Because, silly, we don't want to get caught. The jail is right down the road. We are walking."

Now I feel like a criminal, like they calling my uncle Buddy. Like thieves in the night, we walk to the jail, ducking behind bushes, stores, and the movie house all the way. Finally we make it to the store next to the jail. Chick-A-Boo ain't saying nothing and I think she is going to cry any minute.

"Now what?" I ask, wanting to cry myself.

"We have to hide and wait," Randy whispers. He is sure something is going to happen. He probably has been ease dropping too.

"Get down!" Randy whispers.

Randy, Chick-A-Boo, and me hide behind the dime store.

No wonder Grandma and Ma never buy anything in this store. It's nasty back here.

"You yell, nigger, and we will kill you!" The words rip through the air. I hope I am back at Grandpa's in the bed dreaming, but this is no dream. Five men with sheets on their head come out of the jailhouse. I have heard Grandpa and Mr. Charlie talk about the Ku Klux Klan a thousand times on the front porch at night, but I never thought I would see them with my own eyes.

I look them over one by one. White sheets and white hoods over their heads, and they all are wearing black shoes. One of them is carrying a shotgun. My uncle Buddy walks out with a look of terror on his face like I have never seen before.

"Move, nigger!" one of them KKK men yells, as he pushes Uncle Buddy in his back with the butt of the shotgun.

My feet move to run.

I have to do something. What, I don't know. But I have to save Uncle Buddy.

Randy pushes me back down.

"Get down before you get us all killed, fool."

"But what about my uncle?"

"We will follow them and see where they take him," says Chick-A-Boo. Peeping back up, we see them forcing Uncle Buddy into the boot of a black car.

Three of them climb inside and the other two get in a car in front of the one with Uncle Buddy, and they all start driving away.

Chick-A-Boo, Randy, and me are now running as fast as we can behind the building, trying to get back to the pickup truck to follow them.

When the two Klan cars get to the end of Main Street, just before you enter Lovers' Lane that leads to the swamp, they get caught at the stoplight. Our only stoplight.

"They stopped," Randy says.

Still on foot, we ease to the end of the building to see which way they are going to turn.

"Stop, or I will shoot!"

Lord, I almost pee on myself again, because I think they have caught us. But no, in between Moore's Grocery and the Fish House, we peep again. All we can see is the back of Uncle Buddy running faster than a jackrabbit. The boot is wide open. I can't believe they didn't tie Uncle Buddy up.

That white trash raises his rifle into the air and aims it at Uncle Buddy. I close my eyes and wait for his head to blow into the night sky.

But the tallest KKK man knocks the attempted murderer's gun to the ground.

"You fool, you are going to wake up all of Main Street!" Thank God, that Klan member has come to his senses. He can't shoot Uncle Buddy, so he lowers his rifle.

They chase Uncle Buddy on foot. We chase them.

Then I hear a big splash and I know my prayers are answered.

He did it. Uncle Buddy just made it to the swamp. All those big fat white men are on their knees out of breath.

We run into the woods so they don't see us.

"Randy, my uncle ain't going to get caught. He and Grandpa hunted in the swamp for rattlesnakes to make belts for years. He knows that swamp, and they aren't going to never find him. Never!"

Good God from Zion.

We laugh. . . .

We laugh. . . .

We laugh. . . .

Out of breath . . .

We laugh. . . .

We are going home.

I climb back in the bedroom window.

Just like I figure, Ma and Grandma are still asleep in the sitting room. I sleep like a newborn baby for the rest of the night.

14

Back to Harlem

*T*his morning I make sure that I am up early enough to ease drop on Grandma and Grandpa while Ma is taking a bath.

"Braxton, where in the world did you go last night?" Grandma asks in a whisper.

"Woman, you know better than to ask Masons' business."

"Masons' business? Man, you got one foot in the grave and the other one on a banana peeling and you talking about don't ask Masons' business?"

Grandpa kind of chuckles at that one. One foot in the grave and the other one on a banana peeling.

That's what she and Uncle Buddy are always saying about Mr. Bay.

"Ain't no need to get all out of place now," says
Grandpa. "I didn't go to Rich Square. The meeting
was at Johnny Williams' house. We met for the
final plans to get Buddy out of jail before them
white folks killed him. The senior Masons stayed
there and played bait with Johnny while some of
the other men folks went off and did what they had
to do."

"Played bait? You best start making sense, Braxton Jones, if you plan to eat breakfast this mornin'."

Poor Grandpa. Now she is controlling him with
food.

"If you hush your fussing, I will tell you the rest.
See, around midnight, we stage for Johnny's brother,
Tradus, to get sick. Then we called the law for
them to come down there to help us. That's the
reason we had the meeting at Johnny's, because he
is the only colored on Bryant Town Road with a
telephone. Of course the law came, because you
know Tradus cleans the jailhouse, and if they like
any colored person in Rich Square, it Tradus. It's

amazing what white folks will do to take care of coloreds that clean their houses and offices.

"Anyway, when they got down there, just as we thought, not only did they take care of Tradus, they took him clean to the hospital in Rocky Mount. Tradus shoo should go out to Hollywood and start acting, because he fooled them white boys."

"Then what happen?"

"What do you think happen?" Grandpa answered.

"The young men folks went to break Buddy out of jail. Had a car waiting to take him to Newport News, then on to Harlem. 'Course they cut through the swamp so white folks wouldn't see them coming to town. Go through the swamp and you don't have to worry about white folks; they think it's filled with hanks and slave bones. Anyway, when the Masons made it deep in the swamp, out of nowhere Buddy jumped. Didn't have to break him out of jail. Never even made it to town. The KKK beat them to Buddy and by God, he got away from them somehow and made it to that swamp.

"That boy knows that swamp like I know Jones

Property. Brother Boone said they met Buddy midway. He was knee-deep in water and they spotted each other at the same time. They told me every word my boy said."

"'Buddy,' Brother Boone yelled.

"'Bro Boone. Yes it's me,' Buddy yelled back.

"'Get over here, man. We were on our way to get you out of jail. How in the sand hill did you get out on your own?' Brother Boone asked.

"Buddy told the Masons how the Klan took him out of jail. After that, they left that swamp and made it to the cars, and Brother Smitty took him on to Newport News. From there they taking him to New York. He must be halfway to Harlem by now."

Grandma drops one of the plates with the dancing white ladies on it.

Better her than me.

"You mean my boy out of jail? Jesus to the highest!"

Grandma throws her hands in the air and starts shouting like she has the Holy Ghost.

"Thank, thank, thank you, Jesus. Oh, thank you, Jesus. I been praying for my child."

This is better than watching a Saturday night movie.

For a moment, I feel the spirit too. Then I realize it's Ma hitting me on my behind with Grandpa's belt.

"Girl, didn't I tell you about ease dropping?"

Grandma is praising the Lord so loud that Ma heard her all the way in the washroom.

Lick one is painful. Lick two is harder, and three and four are worse. Five, I feel like hell has come to earth.

"Go and put your Sunday clothes on," Ma says in between licks.

I want to cry, but I have made up my mind that almost-teenagers don't cry. So I hang on to Ma's waist so that every time she hit me, she hits herself too. Well, that is a mistake.

She stops and now she is giving me the look of death.

"You have finally lost your mind! Go to your room and put your clothes on. You ain't going nowhere but to the fields for the rest of the summer!"

I am not going to look at her. Surely, she don't mean I can't go to Harlem. But this is no time to ask. I run to my room and close the door. Grandpa and Grandma never even heard me getting my tail whipped because Grandma is still calling on the Lord.

I dress for church.

Chapel Hill Baptist Church ain't going to be able to hold the folks today.

When we drive up, the deaconesses have posted signs on every tree on the church ground.

"Buddy Bush is free. Thank God."

Sore behind and all, Lord what a time we have.

15

The Law

*I*t's Monday morning and I'm back in the fields.

Everyone in the fields are talking about my uncle Buddy Bush escape. And the law is all over Rich Square looking for him. Randy said they are bringing in some outside law, from over in Potecasi.

Chick-A-Boo and me are staying close to each other all day and we ain't talking very much to nobody else. I don't even talk to Miss Nora all day. We have witnessed a crime and we are scared to death. Randy acts like nothing even happen on Saturday night.

"Who's that?" Chick-A-Boo asks.

I look up and see something that scares me worse than what we saw two nights ago.

A white truck with a bunch of white men on the back. Who are they and what do they want? White folks only come on Rehobeth Road if they own land or to see Mr. Bay.

We aren't moving a inch as the white men raise shotguns in the air and yell, "We want that nigger, Buddy Bush!"

"A nigger for a white woman!"

"Keep chopping. Don't look up," Randy orders.

Randy ain't afraid of them, or at least he ain't showing it.

We do as we are told and the white men keep going.

When they are out of sight, Randy stops chopping.

"This ain't over. We better get out of here."

We take our hoes to the end of the field to put them where we always do.

"Don't leave nothing out here. We can't work like this. It's too dangerous."

I want to be there when Randy tells Ole Man Taylor that we ain't chopping today. The truth be told, Ole Man Taylor might be glad, because the last thing he needs is bloodshed on his land.

When Randy drops me off, I am so glad to get home. I am tired. Tired from being out all Saturday night. Tired from the whipping I got yesterday morning, and tired from chopping weeds out of white folks' cotton till noon today. I don't even remember eating supper, taking a bath, or going to bed.

The law wakes me this morning. Knocking on the door like they crazy. Before my feet can touch the floor, Grandma is at the front door.

"Stop banging on my door."

"Open up."

"Open up for who?" she yells back.

"It's me, Sheriff Franklin, and my deputies, Paul and Bill."

"Didn't I tell you never to step on Jones Property again?"

Old Sheriff Franklin must have forgotten that

thirty-five years ago Grandma promised him a bullet for hitting Grandpa over the head. Of course, I have made it to the keyhole in time to witness Ma stop Grandma from killing them lawmen.

"It's me, Mer, Sheriff. How can I help you?"

"You know how you can help me. We looking for that brother of yours. Now open up!"

"He ain't here. Now, unless you got a search warrant, I can't let you in."

"Gal, you better open this door."

Wrong answer! Grandma is furious. She swings the door open, almost knocking the white man down.

"Get off my damn porch!" Grandma yells.

Uncle Buddy is right. If you own your own house, you really can say, "Get off my damn porch."

I believe old Sheriff Franklin just got his memory back right this second. I run to the door in time to see only the back of the sheriff's head as he jumps off the porch.

"I'll be back with a search warrant."

"Damn if you will," Grandma shouts.

Yeah for Grandma. She ain't scared of no white folks and she done lost her religion. She best get to church first come Sunday morning.

Ma is shocked at Grandma. Me, I am too happy.

"Lord, Ma, you can't talk to white folks like that, especially the law."

"This is my house, mine and Braxton. Ain't no law coming in here. Buddy gone and he gone for good."

"That may be so, but he's done ran from the law and they coming back. Please let them in so Poppa won't be upset."

"Upset? Braxton lying in there on his deathbed now because of that Sheriff Franklin. He almost killed him thirty-five years ago, now he trying to kill our boy."

Grandpa hears all the noise and slowly walks to the sitting room.

"Babe, what in the world is going on?"

"Poppa, the law came by looking for Bro, and Ma Babe she . . ."

Ma is thinking before she says another word.

I swear I think Grandma might slap a grown

woman with children down if Ma do say something else.

"All right, all right, settle down, women folks, 'cause they will be back. He ain't here, so it don't matter. When they do come back, let them in." Grandpa has spoken.

He turns and walks away.

With all their mouthing and controlling, them women know not to mess with my grandpa. Ma goes about her morning courses; Grandma mouths a few words and goes back to cooking breakfast.

Me, I just laugh. To myself, of course.

I'm just glad to be out of the fields again. I get dressed and go back on the front porch and wait for the law to return.

In less than thirty minutes they are back.

"Here they come, Ma. Here they come," I yell.

I almost turn over in Grandpa's rocking chair. Waiting for the law is a lot of stress on a twelve-year-old.

Ma and Grandma meet the law at the door. Grandpa gathers enough strength to get to the door before Grandma shoot anybody.

"Sheriff Franklin," Grandpa says with authority.

"Mr. Braxton, I came to search your house for your boy. Right here is the search warrant."

"Don't need to see that paper. Come in and do what you got to do."

"Mind stepping outside while we look around?"

Grandpa turns to Ma.

"I do mind. Mer, read that search warrant. If it don't say we got to go outside, tell me so."

Ma, with her smart self, reads that search warrant in less than a minute. "Poppa, it don't say that."

"Fine, we staying. Now Mer, you and Pattie Mae go with them in every single room."

Sheriff Franklin is too mad.

"Mr. Braxton, we prefer you go outside."

"Sheriff, I prefer if you weren't here at all. Now do your business and leave. Unless you plan to knock me out like you did thirty-five years ago, me and my folks ain't going nowhere."

He don't even wait for the law to respond. He turns and walks away with all that Jones pride glowing through his old feeble body.

Grandma turns and walks away with a gun in her apron pocket.

Ma and me take our positions.

When they move to the left, we do too.

To the right—we do too.

The kitchen; us too.

The sitting room; us too.

This goes on for an hour.

Right through lunchtime.

But who is hungry?

Finally Deputy Paul says, "He ain't here, boss."

Ma impolitely says, "I told you that an hour ago."

They gather their stupidity and out the door they go.

Ma starts putting the house back in order and Grandma helps.

Grandpa takes his midday nap after they leave and I go back to my position on the front porch, just in case they return.

When they are out of sight, I make my announcement.

"They gone, y'all."

Ma shouts back, "Come in this house, child, and peel some potatoes for supper."

16

Have You Ever Seen Cotton Grow?

Supper sure smells good. We are eating early tonight because we skipped lunch. Chicken pot pie, greens, potatoes, iced tea, and, of course, strawberries for dessert.

Just as Grandpa is about to pray, someone knocks at the back door next to the kitchen. It's Mr. Bay. According to Grandpa, he ain't stepped foot on this land since it belonged to Wynter Waters. Grandpa said he was so prejudice that if Sue never drops another glass of milk, we wouldn't buy any from Mr. Bay.

Grandpa speaks to him first. "Evening, Bay. What can I do for you?"

"Evening, Braxton. I got today's paper and I thought you might want to read what they saying about your boy."

"I do," Grandpa says with grace.

"I'll just leave it right here."

He lays the paper on the back doorstep and starts to walk away.

I leave the table to pick up the paper. Mr. Bay stops again, like someone has shot him. He turns around and looks in our faces like he has never seen us before.

I freeze at the door, realizing this is the closest I have ever got to his white face. It looks so kind. Nothing like I thought. Almost as kind as Grandpa's.

"If it means anything, I want y'all to know that I don't believe any of that mess they saying about your boy."

Grandma smiles for the first time in weeks.

A tear runs down Grandpa's face.

Ma weeps like she did at June Bug's funeral.

"Thank you, Mr. Bay," I say as he walks away.

A white man has made us feel better.

It's TV time, but not tonight. Ma tells me to get that paper and read it to them. We sit in Grandma and Grandpa's bedroom so Grandpa can lie down while I read the article to them.

It's not just any article.

It's front-page news.

GOODWIN "BUDDY" BUSH WANTED

This male Negro escaped from the authorities on July 10, 1947. He is wanted for the attempted rape of an unnamed white woman in Rich Square, North Carolina. If anyone sees him, please contact your local authorities immediately.

Next to those painful words is a picture of Uncle Buddy.

A big picture.

That picture and those words, surely, are the end of Grandpa.

His heart is broken.

I don't think Grandpa is ever going to get out of

that bed again. His yellow skin turns blue and green and Grandma has to change him like he is a baby. He mourns and calls for Uncle Buddy night and day. Grandpa don't want to see Dr. Franklin. Don't want him on Jones Property. So last night we call the new colored doctor from Potecasi to come over. Yes, we got our colored doctor after all. Dr. Grant shows up 9 o'clock this morning. I don't know what colored doctors are supposed to look like, but he is dressed like he is on his way to Sunday go to meeting. He has his doctor's bag and bad, bad news. He announces that Grandpa will be dead before the cotton bloom.

Before the cotton bloom. If you ain't never seen cotton grow, you don't understand. Lord, when it's ready it's just like the babies Grandma delivers. They just pop out.

"Before the cotton bloom," I scream and run to Mer's tree. It seems like all twelve years of my life are running behind me. Hobo run too. I cry. Hobo is making weeping noises like he did when Randy hit him with a beebee gun last year.

It is a long day and Ma cries late into the night.

Hudson is sleeping under the bed, like he has all my life. Grandma ain't doing much crying. She just keep praying the Lord's Prayer.

After the colored doctor's visit, Mr. Charlie starts coming by earlier each day and staying late. Sometime he sits on the porch all alone. Other times he just pulls a chair up to Grandpa's bed and they look at each other for hours. Miss Doleebuck comes two and three times a day, armored with hugs, kisses, and food. They try to comfort us, but nothing can change what is happening on Jones Property since the colored doctor came. The cotton has started to change. The bulbs that use to be green and soft are turning brown and hard. They will soon bloom and death will come on in. Folks on Rehobeth Road say a cat can sense death before people can. So I keep a close eye on Hudson. Today is the fifth of August and I wake up and can't find him nowhere. I run to the smokehouse. No Hudson.

I run to Mer's tree.

Buddy's tree.

Rosie's tree.

Louise's tree.

No Hudson.

Me and Hobo look everywhere on Jones Property. No Hudson. Then we run to the slave house. I run around back to the tree that Hudson likes to sit in when he comes home with me. Hudson's not here, but something is wrong with this tree. The bell. Mr. Spivey done stole the bell. Wait till I tell Ma. What am I saying? I don't care about that bell or Mr. Spivey. I have to find Hudson. I run through the cucumber patch that is filled with weeds because we been gone most of the summer. Ma comes here every few days while Grandpa is asleep, long enough to get the new cucumbers, but she don't have time to chop the weeds out, too. Down the rows I run until I reach Ole Man Taylor's cotton field next to the woods. "God, no." I see the white soft cotton trying to come out. "No-o-o-o-o-o-o-o. Not yet, Grandpa, it's too soon! The cotton ain't out yet. Just a little bit." I start running back down Rehobeth Road, back to Jones Property. I run hard, but it's too late. I open the door to where Grandpa is surely dying.

"Babe," he says. "I'm so tired; you take care of yourself. Mer, you take care of Jones Property, take care of your mama, and my grandbaby."

Still managing to smile as he walks to the valley of the shadow of death, just like Reverend Wiggins said folks do when they dying. "Pattie Mae, you in charge now."

Then he closes his eyes and heads on to heaven. Grandpa's last breath feels like forever before, right in Ma's arms, he dies. If I live to be one hundred years old, I will never forget her scream.

I can't cry because I have cried every day since Dr. Grant left. So I just stand there and watch the only daddy I ever had slip away.

Grandma strong. She ain't shedding any tears. She reach down and separates his body from Ma's and lays Grandpa back on the bed. His eyes are still open until Grandma closes them. Then she pulls the sheet over his head.

"Call Joe Gordon," she says to me.

I run to the phone and call the black undertaker.

Didn't nobody tell me to, but I'm calling Bar-Jean.

"He's gone, sister."

She lets out a scream louder than Ma did.

In between screams, she says, "I'll be home soon as y'all know the funeral date."

I hang up and don't call nobody else. That is BarJean's duty to call all the kinfolks up North when something goes wrong on Rehobeth Road.

Without Grandma telling me, I run as fast as I can to get Mr. Charlie. I see him from the road. He is sitting on his front porch, carving a piece of wood.

"Mr. Charlie, Mr. Charlie, come quick!"

He stops carving and stands up.

He knows his best friend in the world is gone. I look down at the wood and it is a doorplate with the word "Jones" on it.

I am still looking down at the wood when Mr. Charlie says, "Did you call Joe Gordon?"

"Yes, sir, I did."

"Rest on, Braxton, rest on," he says like he is giving Grandpa permission to die.

Miss Doleebuck comes on the porch.

"Is he gone, child?" she ask in between tears.

"Yes ma'am, he gone."

Mr. Charlie lays his wood and knife down and gets his walking stick. Miss Doleebuck hugs me and takes my hand.

Together we walk back across Mr. Charlie's yard, across Rehobeth Road, on to Jones Property. Grandma has quickly changed into a black dress. She is going in every room covering the mirrors with clean white sheets. The women on Rehobeth Road believe that it's bad luck to look at yourself when someone in the house is dead, but not buried. I don't know if that's so, but I know we didn't look at ourselves for a week when June Bug drowned.

"Now, Pattie Mae, don't touch a mirror on Jones Property until after the funeral."

"I wouldn't, Grandma."

Grandma has closed the door where Grandpa is now. And we all go and sit on the porch, waiting for Joe Gordon. Everybody except Mr. Charlie. He leans on the closed door like he can't move. Even in death he is standing by his best friend.

It don't take long for Mr. Gordon to get here in his white hearse with two other men. Now I am crying. Crying because I know when they leave, things will never be the same here. I sit in Grandpa's rocking chair until I hear Mr. Gordon at the front door.

When they come out, they have my grandpa. I can see his hand from under the sheet. I stand up and touch his hand. I hold it and I don't want to let go. It is still so warm, like his kisses. Ma pulls me away and they are leaving with Grandpa. He is leaving Jones Property for the last time. The place he worked for. A place for Ma. A place for Uncle Buddy. A place for me. Slowly they take Grandpa down the steps.

"Grandpa, come back!" I scream and run in the house.

What will I do now? Grandpa gone to heaven and Uncle Buddy can't ever come home again.

It doesn't take long for folks to realize Grandpa done gone to meet his maker. The house is full of folks. They pray and bring pies, cakes, you name it.

Mr. Gordon sends two men to get about twenty chairs for the guests to sit in. They bring a dead folks' wreath and hang it on the door. Folks just keep coming throughout the day and evening. I am sick of them by nightfall and I go to bed early. I can't sleep and I hear so many voices—Miss Thelma, Miss Blanche, Miss Nora, and a lot of other people.

Grandma has decided we will bury Grandpa next Saturday and folks start spreading the word. All week, the women folks work on the funeral arrangements. Everyone from up North are coming today by train. Aunt Rosie, Aunt Louise, Irene, and kinfolks that I have never seen before. BarJean and Coy ain't coming by train. They driving Coy's new car.

A Cadillac.

A blue Cadillac.

Uncle Buddy would be tickled.

Friday evening seems to take forever as we get ready for the sittin' up. Joe Gordon drives up with his helpers and they take Grandpa's body out of the hearse. So I was wrong last week when I thought Grandpa would never be on Jones Property again. I forgot that on Rehobeth Road when someone dies, the night before the funeral, Mr. Gordon brings the body back to spend the night.

They bring Grandpa's body back in a coffin that he paid for ten years ago. The brown wood is shining like Uncle Buddy's shoes used to.

I just stand there as they set the coffin down in the sitting room like it is a piece of furniture from Sears. Mr. Gordon does the job of opening the casket so that folks can see Grandpa. They start going in a few at a time to sit with Grandpa and talk about how much they liked him. But not Mr. Charlie. He ain't leaving that coffin. He sit there all night, even when Grandma is not in the room. I only go in that dark room one time.

Grandpa don't really look dead. Just asleep.

I finally go to bed and I sleep off and on, knowing my grandpa is dead in the room next to me. I just can't imagine this house, this life of mine without him.

Grandpa's rooster sound so different this morning, but I'm up to the sound of his crowing. Two hours later Mr. Gordon is back to pick up the coffin in the hearse for the funeral, and I leave the house. Down to our favorite tree I walk. Mer's tree. I already watched them take my grandpa last week. I can't bear to watch them take him again.

It ain't long before Ma sends Coy to get me because we will be leaving soon for the funeral.

I don't want to be a flower girl. Uncle Buddy said flower girls make funerals look like weddings. BarJean is a flower girl and Coy is a pallbearer. Everyone is wearing black except me. I'm wearing my outfit that I wore to the picture show with Uncle Buddy.

Poor Uncle Buddy. I wonder if he got word about Grandpa. I hope not, because he can't come back here anyway.

After they put Grandpa in the hearse, Mr. Gordon starts to arrange the funeral line. We have to line up in the order of kin.

I bet if Uncle Buddy were here, no one would care about blood kin. We line up in twos as Mr. Gordon calls for us.

Miss Babe Jones.

Daughters.

Grandchildren.

Nieces.

Nephew.

He calls every kinfolk one would think of,
except son. The only son Grandpa ever had is out
there on the run somewhere. As we pulls off, I look
out the car window and there he is. It's Hudson.
He's back. He jumps in Grandpa's rocking chair
and I swear every hair on his back stands up. I ain't
telling nobody what I just saw. Nobody!

When we get to the church, we get out of the
family cars slower than we got in. Our time with
Grandpa is almost over. The church bell rings just
as we walk inside. Reverend Wiggins leads us in.

The choir sings "May the Work I've Done Speak
for Me" first.

Everybody in Rich Square is here for Grandpa's
funeral. Even a few white folks are here: Ole Man
Taylor, Mr. and Mrs. Wilson, and Mr. Bay.

But not one Franklin. They know better than to
show their faces.

Mr. Charlie stands up to say a few words about

my grandpa. His tears look like they are connected to a string, they are coming so fast.

I look in every face, looking for Uncle Buddy to come in, hiding under a hat. Of course, Miss Nora is here, and she is crying a lot.

You ain't never seen so many flowers at a funeral before in your life. "Give me flowers while I can smell them," Grandpa always said when I would pick him buttercups to put in his shirt pocket. He was just trying to tell me to be nice to people. "Tell them you love them."

I love you, Grandpa. We all love Grandpa.

I keep looking for Uncle Buddy. When the choir start to sing "Precious Lord," I stop thinking about Uncle Buddy and cry until service is over. Aunt Rosie, Ma, and Louise cry the whole service, too. Except when William Spencer Creecy speaks. Mr. Creecy speaks at every funeral. I don't think folks in Rich Square believe a colored person is dead if Mr. Creecy don't say a few words. He has been the principal here at Creecy School and the funeral speaker ever since Ma was a little girl. He says for us not to cry. "The same train that came and got

Brother Braxton will be back for you," he declares.

There!

It is official: Grandpa is dead.

We lay Grandpa to rest right beside June Bug in the colored folks' cemetery next to the cotton field. Then we leave him there in that lonely ground and go back to Jones Property.

It raining so hard we are wet from head to toe when we finally make it home.

Miss Doleebuck says, "If it rains the day of a funeral, the Lord is washing someone's soul to heaven." Chick-A-Boo is here holding my hand, but she don't say much. This girl finally figured out when to shut up. She just stand at the window with me and watch the rain. I wonder how long it will take for Grandpa's soul to get to heaven.

Ma and her sisters are talking to all the folks that I wish would go home. Miss Nora is here and she is mostly talking to me now. She says she staying here in Rich Square. She says she have to work in the fields the rest of her life, she ain't going to let white folks run her off unless Uncle Buddy sends for her. After all they done to Uncle Buddy, she is staying. Miss Nora says it ain't nowhere else to go with no money and no education. Ma hugs her and Grandma does too. I can tell they really like Miss Nora.

When everybody leaves, Grandma takes the sheets off the mirrors and announces that we are going on with life.

"Now, Braxton wouldn't want us to grieve long. We got to keep on going."

No sooner than the words are out of Grandma's mouth, Ma makes her own announcement: "Pattie Mae, next week I'm sending you back to Harlem with BarJean. That will give me, Ma, and my sisters time to take care of Poppa's business."

I can't believe it. I'm finally going North. But it's not like I thought my send-off would be. Grandpa isn't here to kiss me good-bye. Uncle Buddy ain't here to tell me how to act when the train stops in Rocky Mount. Harlem don't seem so sweet no more.

17

The Train

I get up early on leaving day. Me, Hudson, and Hobo go over and say bye to Miss Doleebuck and Mr. Charlie. Then we walk down the road and say good-bye to the Edward children. Chick-A-Boo is crying like she really is going to miss me. I know I am going to miss her some kind of bad.

Coy drives us to the train station. He is staying down South a few more days to do the driving for the women folks. Mr. Charlie's blood pressure has been too high since Grandpa died; Dr. Grant says he can't drive right now.

"You be a big girl now," Coy says as I climb out of his car.

Ma hugs me and kiss all of her lipstick off onto my face. Grandma never moves from the front seat. She just waves and tries not to let me see her cry.

"See y'all in two weeks," I yell as they drive off.

BarJean pulls my hair.

"Now, don't say 'y'all' in Harlem."

We laugh.

It feels good to laugh.

This train is much bigger than I thought. The conductor looks just like I knew he would. Tall and white, with a funny-looking hat on.

"All aboard!" he yells like Grandma used to yell at Grandpa and me. I gather my two suitcases with most the clothes I have in the world in them, and get on the train. The train I have waited for as long as I can remember.

"Can I sit at the window?" I ask BarJean as we walk down the aisle.

"Yes, you can."

I sit down with ease.

I am suppose to be happy.

But I want to jump off the train and run to the cemetery and dig up my grandpa, so that I can hold him one more time. Maybe if I run back to the swamp, I can find Uncle Buddy.

"I'll get us a soda pop," BarJean announces, as I get lost in my thoughts. I look up and the old lady across from me is smiling with the one tooth she has. She has on her Sunday go to meeting clothes. With serious, serious eyes like Grandma. They look into mine.

"Child, what's ailing you?"

"Just thinking about life."

"Life? Child, you ain't old enough to think about life. Where you from?"

"I'm from Rich Square. Where are you from?"

"Florida, and I have been riding all night. These old knees of mine hurt some kind of bad."

Those serious eyes look right through me.

"Did you say you were from Rich Square?"

"Yes, ma'am, I did."

"I been reading about that place. They must be some prejudice white law folks there, the way they treated that boy, Buddy Bush."

I can't believe this. All the way in Florida, people know about my uncle.

"Miss, you know about Buddy Bush?"

"Child, everybody that can read know about that boy. He the one who got away from the Klan. It's about time somebody outsmarted them."

She just laughs like she know something that I don't.

"Do you know Buddy Bush, child?"

"Yes, I do."

"Honey, if he ever come back to Rich Square, tell him that this old lady glad he got away."

"I will, I will!" I turn my head and look out the window. For miles all you can see is cotton fields. White as the pure undriven snow. Then I close my eyes to pretend I am asleep. I see Uncle Buddy's face, his smile. I see Grandpa. I want to go back home and things be like they used to be.

At the funeral, Reverend Wiggins said we will surely see Grandpa again. Until then, I just imagine him up there with the cloud heads, with the angels. And maybe, just maybe, I will run into Uncle Buddy in Harlem.

Author's Note

The Legend of Buddy Bush is indeed a labor of love. Let me first say that I have never met Buddy Bush. He came into my life through the voice of my grandmother telling his story over and over on her front porch, on Jones Property night after night when I was a little girl. No, she did not raise him after his mother died. I doubt if she even knew him, other than his name.

In the beginning I was trying to write two novels: one about my family and a second one about Buddy Bush. They soon became one story of a surviving people that emerged into a summer of fun, honor, death, and love. There may be people at home who remember Buddy Bush and know what really happened, and this note is to let readers know that he was a real man who is a part of American history.

Beyond the fiction of this novel, Goodwin "Buddy" Bush was a Rich Square native who worked at the sawmill in Rich Square. His real parents were from George, North Carolina, a little unincorporated town two miles north of Rich Square.

His story began one night in 1947 when he was waiting for his date to get off work. Trying to pass the time away, he sat down on the ground and started fooling with a few rocks. Margaret Allen Bryant, also a Rich Square native and newly separated from her husband, walked past Buddy as she was leaving the beauty salon. Knowing better than to get too close to a strange white woman, he stood up to let her by. She took his gesture as an attempted attack. Upset by her reaction and her scream, he went to the local Myers Theatre without his date and watched the movie alone. After the movie was over he met his date at the local ice cream parlor, where they sat eating together. Within minutes the local sheriff came to arrest Buddy, who had simply moved to let Margaret Allen Bryant pass.

Word spread quietly throughout the black and white community that Buddy had been arrested for trying to rape a white woman. Black people were afraid for him, and white people were outraged by what they assumed he had done.

The horror of that night was just the beginning of what would become the most talked and written about event that ever happened in Northampton County. In May 1947, seven white men with white towels from the local barbershop over their heads went to the county jail in Jackson and took Buddy Bush from his cell. Into the dark night they drove off, after putting him in the trunk of their car. Within a mile of his capture, Buddy Bush jumped from the unlocked trunk and ran for his life. One of the kidnappers ran behind him, firing a single bullet that Buddy Bush later described as "a bullet flying past my head."

For two days, he hid in the swamps, until he

finally made his way back to Rich Square, where he found W. S. Creecy, the local principal, and minister P. A. Bishop to help him. Those two brave African American men drove him to Norfolk, Virginia, for safekeeping. While they were hiding Buddy, the local sheriff and half of the white people in Rich Square were hunting him down like an animal. The newspapers began to write about the incident, and within a few weeks the newspapers were printing articles about an attempted lynching in Rich Square. This publicity forced Sheriff Frank Outland to arrest the seven white men involved, which outraged the white community.

With Buddy still a wanted man, Creecy and Bishop brought him back to the Jackson Jail, after working out a plan for protection with the sheriff. Buddy was then transferred to Central Prison in Raleigh, North Carolina, for safekeeping. This incident was so far out of the sheriff's control now that North Carolina Governor R. Gregg Cherry and FBI director J. Edgar Hoover became involved and sent in the State Bureau of Investigation (SBI) and the FBI to Rich Square to investigate. The story had become an international one, making the London *Times*.

After a very short trial, all seven white men were acquitted, and so was Buddy Bush.

Embarrassed by the injustice of the trial, Governor Cherry called for a retrial, and two of the seven men were arrested again. After a second acquittal, knowing justice would never be served, Buddy Bush left Rich Square for good.

Somehow, the fact that Buddy Bush came back for two trials and the fact that this was an international case was secondary to the black folks in Rich Square. It didn't matter then and, to those who remember, it doesn't matter now. They have one story, and the only one that matters to them: "Buddy got away."

Grandpa's barn

Babe Jones
(Grandma)

Jones Property

Jackson County
Courthouse

Braxton Jones
(Grandpa)

Buddy Bush
and
P. A. Bishop

Acknowledgments

Mothers are our earthly gods. This book is possible only because of God's grace and the prayers of my mother, Maless Moses. I thank her and my nine siblings—Barbara, Daniel, Johnny, Scarlett, Larry, Leon, Loraine, Gayle, and Jackie— for all the joy they have given me.

I am grateful to my extended family: April Russell; Deborah Rogers; the Abnatha family; Sonia Sanchez; Karen Tangora; Pat and Jack Shea; Lennie and Felicia Joyner; Morgan Freeman; Trenise Pots; Darryl, Elliott, Eric, and Trelita Goins; Michael and Chloe Rowell; Xernona Clayton;

Jeffery Baurmind; Wanda and Lauren Linden; Dick Gregory; Shelia Frazier; Barbara Austin; Paul Benjamin; Bill Duke; Randy Glover; Kim Miller; Sharian Williamson; Mr. and Mrs. William Creecy; and Pastor William Sheals.

There are no words in the dictionary to express my gratitude to my attorney and friend, Darryl Miller, and the entire staff at Miller and Pliakas. Special, special thanks to Eric Goins, who read this book over and over to help get it right. The wind beneath the wings of this novel is my editor, Emma Dryden. I am forever grateful to her and to everyone at Simon & Schuster for understanding the voices of my ancestors. Thanks so much to Laquita Green, Pauline Delotach, and Maggie Taylor, who works at the Northampton County Courthouse, where the Buddy Bush trial took place more than fifty years ago.

Thank you, Janice Bubb, who gave me access to the Northampton County Museum and the original articles about Buddy Bush.

Last but not least, I am grateful to my ancestors for giving me this story to tell, and to my beloved friend and mentor, Willie Stargell, who told me fourteen years ago to write this novel. It is written in your memory.

God Bless you all. . . .